CH00545000

A RUI
in t
JUNGLE

A RUMBLE
in the
JUNGLE

by
A Zebra

Illustrated by Cathy Dineen

WOLFHOUND PRESS

© 1989 A Zebra
Illustrations © Wolfhound Press

First published 1989 by
WOLFHOUND PRESS,
68 Mountjoy Square,
Dublin 1.

All rights reserved. No part of this book may be reproduced or utilised in
any form or by any means, electronic or mechanical, including photo-
graphy, filming, recording, video recording, photocopying or by any
information storage and retrieval system, or shall not by way of trade or
otherwise be lent, resold, or otherwise circulated in any form of binding
or cover other than that in which it is published, without prior permission
in writing from the publisher.

Wolfhound Press receives financial assistance from
The Arts Council (An Chomhairle Ealaíon), Dublin, Ireland.

British Library Cataloguing in Publication Data
Zebra, A
    A rumble in the jungle.
    I. Title
    823'.914 [J]

    ISBN 0-86327-240-1

Cover design: S. Cashman
Cover illustration: Cathy Dineen
Typesetting: Redsetter Ltd., Dublin.
Printed by TechMan Ltd., Dublin.

CONTENTS

1

Zebra Gumption

'It isn't fair,' the Lo-clas monkey called Mo-Li cried, her pink lips drawn back to show strong yellow teeth. 'It should be my family who get the house, not her. We are next in line to be housed. We've waited so long. We need the house more than she does.' She glared at the zebra, Chu-lain, her bright brown eyes glistening with anger. 'It's just because she is a Ru-clas, and the niece of a Law Leopard. She's not even mated. It's just not fair,' she repeated, picking a tiny tick from her pale belly and popping it into her mouth.

The wind gusting down the valley of Cal-don in Allegoria was growing stronger. Dark clouds, heavy with rain, were nudging the mountain tops. Soon the clouds would drift down into the jungle valley and disgorge their yearly deluge.

The wise young zebra Chu-lain whinnied angrily, shaking his striped head up and down as he looked at the inscrutable face of Mo-li's mate, Ja-no.

Above him, swinging by their long tails from the branches of a banana tree, four of Ja-no and Mo-li's young were eating bananas. Two smaller babies sat on the dry leafy ground at their parents' feet, picking ticks from each other's hairy bodies. With their tiny wrinkled forefingers and thumbs they cracked open the insects. Then they examined them before eating them.

'Chu-lain,' Ja-no whispered worriedly, 'What do you think we should do? We just can't let the jungle Lords get away with this.'

Chu-lain sighed, then turned away from Ja-no to look down the valley. The river was meandering slowly through the trees. Soon it would be in full flood. Turning back to Ja-no he said, 'I don't know what you can do, Ja-no. If the house has been given to this leopard female, then I'm afraid it's too late.'

Ja-no looked at Mo-li. She had tears in her eyes. Tenderly he put a comforting hairy arm around her shoulders. Chu-lain sighed again. Why did it always have to be him they came to? Why did he have to have the GUMPTION?

As if reading his mind, Mo-li roughly pushed Ja-no's arm away and cried: 'But Chu-lain, you are wise. You have the GUMPTION. Only you can help us. Please . . . please you have to help us. The rains will come soon. We have nowhere to live. We will all perish . . . '

Bending his muscled and striped neck, Chu-lain stared unseeingly at his two front hooves. His big dark eyes glistened. Then, raising his head again, he looked at the monkey Mo-li and whispered sadly, 'I wish I knew how I could help you. I really do . . . . ' Suddenly his anger came like a bolt of lightning, and with his anger came more GUMPTION and a great determination to see this family of monkeys housed. Whinnying loudly, he rose on his two hindlegs, startling Ja-no and Mo-li and frightening their youngest babies who began to cry. 'No!' Chu-lain shouted. 'No. This time they will not get away with it. No . . . it is time . . . . '

As he pawed angrily at the air the four young monkeys in the banana tree stopped eating. Throwing banana skins over their shoulders, they then dropped to the ground, gathered around their parents and stared at the zebra.

'Where is this house?' shouted Chu-lain, his mane standing straight up. 'Show it to me.'

Ja-no gulped. He had never seen a zebra so angry. 'It . . . it isn't very far from here,' he stammered.

'Then take me to it . . . NOW!'

Ja-no turned to Mo-li, who nodded, then bent and scooped up her two younger babies. They immediately stopped crying and snuggled into her hairy chest. Seconds later, the monkey family and the zebra Chu-lain were hurrying noisily through the trees. High above them several hummingbirds spread the news about what was happening. Soon, more and more monkeys began to follow Ja-no, Mo-li and Chu-lain.

As they hurried along the jungle path, chattering excitedly, they were unaware that two sleek Law Leopards were watching them from the undergrowth.

'It's a march,' hissed one. 'A forbidden march, and look who's leading it. That troublesome zebra, Chu-lain. Ha, ha. This time he will get his comeuppance.'

The Law Leopard who had spoken was called Stat. He had a long thin face and a scraggly spotted tail. His companion was called Soet, and he too was thin faced, but several of his teeth were missing.

As Soet watched, hissing angrily, his sharp claws raked deep into the soft bark of a rubber tree. 'Shhh. Come on. Let's see what they're up to. Come on,' he growled. 'And be quiet. We don't want them to spot us.' He turned to wait for Stat. 'Oh come on, Stat,' he snarled. 'Do hurry up.'

'Hold on . . . hold on . . . I'm coming,' Stat growled, bounding noisily after him.

'Be quiet,' snarled Soet. 'They'll hear us . . . '

Keeping a little distance behind Chu-lain and the monkeys, the Law Leopards slipped stealthily after them.

Ja-no and Mo-li led Chu-lain and the others to a clearing as large as a football pitch. On the edge of the clearing hundreds of houses built with saplings, thick branches and broad leaves had their doors facing towards the centre, where many young Lo-clas and Ru-clas were playing together. To his left Chu-lain saw about fifty baby anteaters clambering up the slippery bark of a dead branch and then in turn sliding down into a pile of soft brown leaves. The tiny tails of the anteaters wagged impatiently as they waited their turn to slide. To Chu-lain's right a group of young hyenas were balancing on a plank of wood laid across a thick round log. This see-saw tipped from side to side as the hyenas, laughing hysterically, kept it rising and falling by jumping on and off. Squealing loudly, other hyenas and several rats, frogs and armadillos were playing chase in and out of a maze of branches, some of which had been discarded by the builders of the last house. The whole clearing was ringing with the sounds of the children, but their happy clamour ceased abruptly when they saw the newcomers. The silence alerted the older animals who lived there. One by one the doors of the houses opened and they appeared. With frowns they watched as Ja-no led Chu-lain across the clearing.

With a trembling hand Ja-no pointed to a partly finished house and said, 'There, that is the house we were to get.'

Snorting, Chu-lain whispered: 'Stay here.' Then he walked right up to the front of the house and stood examining it. It only needs a few more branches and a good coating of coconut leaves to make it habitable, he thought. Going to the side of the house, he poked his head through the window and looked inside. Aye, it wouldn't take much to put it right. When he pulled his head out of the window and turned round he saw nearly all the animals who lived in the clearing had gathered.

Some of the anteater adults were sniffing angrily and several hyenas had begun to snap wickedly at the monkeys.

'What do you want with that house?' an adult hyena laughed angrily. 'It has been given to a female leopard.'

Ignoring the hyena, Chu-lain spoke quickly to Ja-no and Mo-li. 'Come, get your family inside. We are going to occupy this house.'

Ja-no gaped at Chu-lain, then looked at his mate. Together they nodded in agreement for, they thought, Chu-lain must know what he is doing. He has the GUMPTION.

'Come, all of you. Inside,' chattered Ja-no, herding his four eldest children towards the house.

'Hurry,' screamed Mo-li. Quickly, carrying her two babies, she followed.

Chu-lain waited for a few moments, then he too pushed inside and closed the door behind him.

All the animals were stunned.

Then one of the anteaters shouted, aghast: 'They're occupying the female leopard's house without permission.'

Some Lo-clas frogs standing beside the anteater croaked to each other whispering, 'They do right to occupy the house. It should have been theirs anyway.'

Murmuring loudly all the animals crowded around the house.

At the edge of the clearing, hidden behind the thick trunks of a group of coconut trees, the Law Leopards growled angrily, their slanted eyes glittering wickedly.

'That is the house my niece was given,' Stat growled.

'Your niece?' Soet hissed, his teeth bared.

'Aye, my niece,' snarled Stat, scraping his extended claws down the wrinkled trunk of a coconut tree.

Now, softly at first, a word whispered by one of the

rats, grew louder and louder, until all the animals, Lo-clas and Ru-clas were chanting it. The word grew and grew into one great roar.

'SQUAT . . . SQUAT . . . SQUAT . . . SQUAT . . . SQUAT . . . .'

Chu-lain stuck his head through the window and shouted over their frenzied roaring, 'Aye, SQUAT. You are right. We'll squat here until we get our rights.'

'SQUATTER . . . DIRTY SQUATTER!' shouted a young hyena, and, picking up a short stick, he threw it at Chu-lain's head.

With a thud the stick struck Chu-lain above his right eye. Whinnying painfully, he pulled his head back inside. As the blood trickled down his striped face and onto his black nose the animals outside began to throw more sticks at the house.

'Get down!' shouted Ja-no, pushing his mate, who was still holding her two babies, onto the floor. 'And stay there.'

'It's time we made our move,' hissed Soet. 'That Chu-lain has really done it now. Squatting indeed. He'll end up in the PIT for sure. The Great Lords won't stand for this. Come on, Stat. Let's break this up.'

Grinning cruelly, the Law Leopards bounded into the clearing. Snarling and hissing angrily, they chased all the animals back to their houses.

'You are all to stay inside,' Stat roared. 'You are not to interfere with the foolish zebra and the Lo-clas monkey family. These squatters will be dealt with by our Great Lords.'

As he said this, several Lo-clas armadillos looking out of the windows of their houses gasped with fear. Then they heard a laughing hyena shout from the safety of his front door, 'The Great Lords better deal with them. That house belongs to a Ru-clas leopardess . . .'

With eight quick leaps, Soet reached the hyena before he had time to shut his door. With a low growl he cuffed the shocked hyena on the ear and knocked him flying. 'Obey the jungle law,' he roared. 'You will not interfere with the squatters. They will be punished. The Great Lords will deal with them. Understand?'

'Aye . . . aye . . . I understand,' laughed the hyena, rubbing his painful ear.

'Good,' growled Soet. 'Now get into your house and stay there or you will be thrown in the PIT.'

When the Law Leopards were sure the clearing was peaceful again, they raced off to report to their commanders. Above them the hummingbirds were carrying the news of what had happened to other parts of Allegoria.

2

The Homeless Monkeys

Three fat tigers, Great Lords, lay snoring under a row of massive mahogany trees. The trunks grew so close together that a smooth wall of wood rose behind and the overhanging branches stretched almost to the ground in front – forming a sheltered hideaway. Beams of sunlight filtering through the branches lit the interior. Lying just inside the hideaway were the remains of an antelope which had been hunted and killed earlier that day. The three tigers' peaceful slumbers were disturbed by a cheetah, who slipped easily under the branches, padded over to the nearest tiger and nudged him with his cold nose.

'Eh? . . . What?' the Tiger Lord snarled angrily: 'Well, what is it? You know I hate being wakened so soon after eating. WELL?' he roared again, his sharp teeth dripping saliva as he glared into his steward's eyes.

His roar awakened the other tigers.

'What is it?' one of them growled, stretching himself.

'Why have you wakened me?' the other Great Lord snarled, glaring at the cheetah.

'There . . . there are th-three Law Leopards ou-outside, your Lordships,' the cheetah stammered. 'They . . . they beg to speak with you. They say it is of the utmost importance.'

'Well, what are you standing there for? Show them

in,' roared the first tiger.

'Right . . . right away, your Lordship,' the cheetah steward said, backing out under the branches.

Seconds later, two nervous Law Leopards and their commander stood before the tigers. Quickly Stat and Soet relayed all that had happened.

'SQUATTING you say. Squatting in Cal-don. A zebra, and a family of monkeys,' roared the first tiger. 'By heavens, they will pay for this. They will pay dearly.'

'Pay,' Soet whispered to Stat, grinning.

'Yes, pay,' another Great Lord snarled. Then glaring at the Leopard Commander, he said, 'Go, do your duty. Throw out these troublemakers. And bring this . . . this Chu-lain to us. This zebra is not the only animal in Allegoria with the GUMPTION. He must be taught a lesson.'

'Aye, your Lordship,' the Leopard Commander said. 'We will bring him here to be punished.'

The third Great Lord narrowed his yellow eyes at this, then he snarled, 'No . . . wait!' Scratching his hairy chin with one of his extended claws, he said, 'Do not bring them here. See that this Lo-clas zebra is humiliated in front of his own kind. See that he is made to look foolish. See to it that all Lo-clas and Ru-clas believe that the zebra has lost his GUMPTION.'

The three Law Leopards frowned and looked puzzled.

Then the Leopard Commander asked, 'How can we do this?'

'Do it! Anyway you can,' roared the first tiger. 'Throw them all out and punish them whatever way you like, only . . . handle it yourselves. Do you understand?'

Again the Law Leopards looked puzzled.

'DO YOU UNDERSTAND?' the three Great Lords roared together.

'Aye . . . aye, we do, your Lord-Lordships,'

stammered the Leopard Commander. 'We do.'

'Then go. But make sure this does not get out of hand.'

'Aye, aye, your Lordships,' the Leopard Commander growled, pushing the other two leopards out before him. 'Do not worry. It won't get out of hand. We will handle it.'

Outside the hideaway the three Law Leopards breathed sighs of relief. Then they hurried away.

When they had gone, one of the tigers tore strips of meat from the dead antelope's leg and snarled, 'Do you think they really understood?'

The fattest and oldest of the Great Lords glared at him for a few seconds, then reached for a lump of bloody meat, rumbling, 'The Commander will understand. The leopards will do as they are told. That is the main thing. But this, this squatting. We will all have to be alert from now on. We will have to watch out for this Chu-lain. He has friends, friends with the GUMPTION, dangerous friends. Yes, we will have to watch out for them all.'

Late that same night, even after Ja-no and Mo-li had managed to get their frightened young to sleep, Chu-lain's head still throbbed with the pain of his injury. Earlier, Mo-li had chewed some tobacco leaves that she had pulled from the roof of the house and had spread the soothing paste over Chu-lain's cut.

'Ja-no, Moli,' Chu-lain whinnied, 'I don't think the Law Leopards will come tonight. They will probably wait until first light. Nevertheless, Ja-no, you and I must take turns to keep watch. I will take the first half of the night. Then you can relieve me.' He smiled at the worried couple, then added softly: 'You must be tired. Go, get some sleep. I will wake you later, Ja-no.'

Ja-no grinned at him, then led Mo-li to the far side of the room.

Now Chu-lain had time to reflect. Yes, he thought, we

have done the right thing. We have. But he trembled as he thought about what would happen in the morning. The Law Leopards will come. They will drag us out, but by then the news will have spread throughout Allegoria. Many other animals will be here in the morning. As the thoughts flooded his mind he found himself humming a tune. An old tune, and the words came easily to him as he now sang softly.

'WE SHALL ALL BE E . . . EQUAL. WE SHALL ALL BE E . . . EQUAL. WE SHALL ALL BE EQUAL SOME DAY . . . AY . . . AY . . . AY . . . AY.'

Ten minutes later he was fast asleep.

*   *   *

The tumultuous noise of thousands of animals gathered in the clearing at Cal-don awoke Chu-lain. Scrambling to his feet, he stared out the window. A great cheer erupted, drowning out the angry jeers of some Ru-clas hyenas. Chu-lain blinked back his tears.

When the cheering subsided, a zebra standing near the front of the crowd rose on his two hindlegs and yelled: 'Power to you, Chu-lain. Power to you.'

At this the crowd cheered again.

Chu-lain smiled grimly as he recognised his friend, Tua-tal. Poking two legs through the window he waved at him.

'We are all behind you, Chu-lain,' Tua-tal shouted. 'Don't worry. No harm will come to you. There are too many of us.'

'Aye . . . aye,' shouted hundreds of monkeys from the branches.

Suddenly all the animals grew quiet. The birds stopped their excited singing and the monkeys swung gently from their tails. The Law Leopards had arrived. Marching into the crowd, they forced their way right up to the front of the house. There were fifty of them. Fifty of the strongest Law Leopards in the jungle. They all carried batons made of the hardest wood. Their four commanders wore halved coconut shells tied to their heads with thin leather thongs.

Chu-lain and the monkey family within held their breath as the Law Leopards were ordered to spread out. When they were in a half-circle, the leader of the battalion of Law Leopards stepped forward. Immediately all the animals behind him began to murmur.

'Quiet! You will all be quiet,' screamed the leader. Holding up a strip of tree bark, he shook it, then roared for everyone to hear. 'I will read this out to the squatters. It is jungle law. They have broken jungle law.' He looked around him, waiting for the noise to die down again. Then he continued. 'You, Chu-lain, a zebra, and Ja-no and Mo-li, monkey parents of six young are accused of squatting.'

'Dirty squatters . . . Yahhh!' screamed several Ru-clas deer. Some of the Lo-clas monkeys glared at them, drawing back their gums in anger.

'It is my duty,' continued the leader, 'to tell you that if you do not leave the house in exactly one hour, you will all be thrown out by force. The Great Lords have commanded this.' Lowering the bark-paper, he glared at Chu-lain. 'You, Chu-lain, because you are supposed to have the GUMPTION, you have committed a very serious crime by breaking jungle law. Not only that, you have encouraged others to break jungle law. Therefore, the Great Lords have ordered me to place you under arrest. You will be thrown in the PIT.'

At this, all the animals, Lo-clas and Ru-clas began to shout: 'No . . . noooooo . . . noooo!'

'Be quiet!' screamed the leader.

Now some Law Leopards began to hit out with their

batons at some monkeys and zebras who were trying to push closer to the house.

Raising the strip of bark again, the leader read on. 'The monkey family will be unharmed, and no further action will be taken against them if they leave the house within the hour.' Then he lowered the bark-paper. 'That is all I have to say. You have one hour.' Suddenly, with a loud snarl, he slashed at the thin bark-paper and tore it to shreds. Then he swung around and walked back to the other leopards.

As he stood at the window with Ja-no and Mo-li, Chu-lain could feel them trembling. What have I done, he thought dismally. What have I done? His own heart pounded with fear as he stared over at Tua-tal who was still standing on his hindlegs waving to him. Dejectedly he waved back, to more cheers from the crowd.

Meanwhile, word of the squatting had spread throughout Allegoria and more and more animals, Ru-clas and Lo-clas were hurrying to Cal-don. Fifty minutes later the noise of a million animals had become deafening. Cal-don was surrounded and the clearing itself was so packed with animals that it was almost impossible to move. The leader of the Law Leopards had already sent for reinforcements. Within minutes, almost one-third of all the Law Leopards in Allegoria were standing ten abreast around the house in a wide half-circle. Clubbing and lashing out with their batons and sharp claws, the Law Leopards tried to hold back all the milling animals.

Meanwhile, Chu-lain spoke quietly to Ja-no and Mo-li. 'You must leave now. I am sorry it did not work out. We did our best. We made our stand, but it was no good. In about five minutes the Law Leopards will break in here and drag us out. You, or some of your young will be injured. I do not want that. The officer said no harm will come to you if you leave within the hour. That hour is almost up.'

'But . . . but, what about you, Chu-lain?' Ja-no cried. 'They will take you away to . . . to . . . the PIT. You will never be seen again . . . .'

Mo-li was crying. With her broad pink lips quivering, she turned away.

'No, Ja-no, they won't throw me in the PIT. There are too many out there to see that they don't. Oh, they might imprison me, and keep me without food for a time, but they daren't harm me. Look, I know this. So please . . . please, leave.'

Nudging her mate, Mo-li with tears in her eyes whispered, 'We will never forget what you did for us, Chu-lain.' Suddenly, with a tiny cry, she leapt up onto Chu-lain's back and, putting her paws around his striped neck, gave him a hug.

Chattering loudly, her four eldest children patted Chu-lain on his heaving side. Ja-no rubbed his nose against Chu-lain's affectionately. Grimly, Chu-lain nodded.

Then Ja-no shouted: 'Come, children, we are leaving . . . come . . . now.'

Jumping nimbly from Chu-lain's back, Mo-li grabbed her two babies and lifted them into her arms. At the door they all turned and looked sadly back at the wise young zebra.

'Thank you again,' Ja-no whispered, then shepherded his family outside.

3

A Peaceful Plan

As they came through the door, a great roar went up and the hummingbirds and parrots in the trees fluttered about happily. Ja-no and Mo-li, their hairy faces streaked with tears, led their young towards the cordon of angry leopards. On a command from their leader, the cordon parted and the monkey family were allowed through. Within seconds they were surrounded by hundreds of monkeys of all kinds.

But the congratulations died down as the final minutes of the hour ticked away. All eyes were on Chu-lain, who was looking through the window.

'You have one minute, zebra. Then we will break in and take you . . . by force,' the Leopard Leader roared.

Chu-lain whinnied angrily. 'You will have to take me by force for I will not leave this house willingly.'

His words were greeted by another loud cheer of encouragement. Chu-lain left the window and put a barricade of branches behind the door.

More animals tried to push their way through the cordon of leopards. Then a few Lo-clas antelopes began to sing. They were joined by Ru-clas deer. Brave Chu-lain almost wept as he heard the song which grew louder and louder.

'WE SHALL ALL BE E . . . EQUAL. WE SHALL ALL BE E . . . EQUAL. WE SHALL ALL BE EQUAL

SOME DAY . . . AY . . . AY . . . AY . . . AY. FOR
DEEP IN OUR HEARTS WE DO BELIEVE, WE
SHALL ALL BE EQUAL SOME DAY . . . '

'Right,' roared the Leopard Leader, stepping forward.
'Your hour is up, zebra.' Turning to the ten nearest
leopards, he snarled, 'You ten, come with me. Tear down
that door.'

Just then, another Leopard Commander pushed
through the cordon to his leader. Growling with anger
the leader listened to what the commander had to say,
then with a quick nod he turned to the ten waiting
leopards.

'I have been informed that the Great Lords do not wish
this zebra, Chu-lain, to be harmed.'

'Not harmed?' growled one of the ten, tearing at the
ground with his sharp claws. 'We can drag him out and
tear him up a bit. Why is he not to be harmed? He has
broken jungle law.'

'Because,' snarled the Leopard Leader, 'it is the Great
Lord's wish, and they must be obeyed. Now, follow me,
and remember the zebra must not be harmed.'

A silence, so still you could hear a coconut drop,
descended on the clearing as the leader led the ten
leopards to the door of the house.

He stepped aside, then growled: 'Tear down the door.'

As the watching crowd saw the ten leopards leap at the
door and rip it to smithereens, they screamed and pushed.
With loud growls the Law Leopards tried to hold them
back.

Now, having smashed the door, the ten leopards stood
back to allow their leader to enter the house first. But on
a quick order they pushed inside before him. Seconds
later they were dragging the struggling Chu-lain outside.

More and more animals pushed forward trying to help
Chu-lain. With loud fearful growls, two Leopard

Commanders left the cordon and ran to their leader.

'We can't hold them back much longer, leader,' one of them whispered fearfully.

'There are too many,' the other commander growled. 'They're out of control. They're not even afraid of us.'

'And they're howling for this Chu-lain to be released. Leader, we cannot hold them back. You will have to let the zebra go or there will be deaths here today.'

His face twisting with rage, the Leopard Leader stared fearlessly at the screaming crowd, watching as his leopards clubbed and ripped at them. He could see his leopards were losing ground. The Great Lords won't like it, he thought. But what can I do? Quickly he made up his mind. Turning to the still-struggling Chu-lain, he snarled, 'If I release you, zebra, you would have to give me your word, your jungle word, that you will never do anything like this again.' He will pay later, he thought, as he watched Chu-lain. 'Well?'

Chu-lain stared at him, then at the angry crowd. Sticks were being thrown now by the monkeys who swarmed in the trees above the houses. Some of the leopards yelped loudly as they were hit. Many will be injured, thought Chu-lain, if I don't give my jungle word. Even as he thought, a plan, a new plan, was already taking seed inside his GUMPTION-filled head.

'Yes, I will give you my jungle word that I will not squat again. But I will not give you my jungle word that I will not protest at the many wrongs I see every day in Allegoria. No, I will not squat again. You have my jungle word on that.'

With a relieved snarl the Leopard Leader ordered the ten leopards holding Chu-lain: 'Release him.'

With puzzled snarls the leopards let Chu-lain go and with a triumphant grin he galloped to the edge of the cordon. Turning, he looked at the leader, who with a loud roar ordered the leopards to allow Chu-lain through. The loudest cheer of the day echoed through the jungle as the brave zebra walked to safety.

'You did it, Chu-lain. Oh you did it,' Tua-tal whinnied joyfully. 'You showed them . . . Ha, ha, ha.' With a great show of emotion he rubbed his nose vigorously against Chu-lain's.

Now many animals crowded around them, congratulating Chu-lain. It was some time before the two zebra friends could make their way out of the clearing.

When they did manage to get away, they galloped along the narrow jungle paths in the direction of their favourite waterhole.

Tua-tal had noticed that Chu-lain was very quiet and looked sad. 'What is it, Chu-lain?' he asked, stopping. 'What's wrong?'

Chu-lain looked at him, his eyes misting up and said, 'Ah, Tua-tal it didn't work. I didn't get Ja-no and Mo-li a house. It was all a waste. It proved nothing. Tua-tal we have to do something more about all the wrongs in Allegoria. Today will soon be forgotten. We must unite all the animals, Lo-clas and Ru-clas. We must make them see that the Great Lords are evil, and they use the Law Leopards to do wrong. We must make all the animals in Allegoria believe that we are all equal.'

Tua-tal studied his friend's serious face for a few moments, then began to whisper excitedly, looking around him to make sure no one could hear him. 'You sound as if you have a plan?'

Chu-lain smiled grimly, then said, 'Maybe I have, Tua-tal. But I will need your help, and Emac's too.'

'What is it, this plan of yours? Tell me,' Tua-tal whispered excitedly as they set off again.

Chu-lain said, 'Let's get to the waterhole first. We'll call a meeting there. By that time I will have worked out the details of my plan.'

One hour later, at the calm waterhole, Chu-lain stood on his hindlegs addressing a group of animals. There were forty Lo-clas zebras there, including the oldest zebra, Emac, whose body was almost completely white. Lo-clas frogs, cranes and armadillos, Ru-clas pink flamingoes, Lo-clas rhinoceroses, all listened intently absorbing every word that Chu-lain spoke.

The animals at the waterhole knew that all meetings such as this were banned by the Great Lords.

'First of all friends,' Chu-lain said, 'I want to thank you for your support today. Ja-no and Mo-li showed great courage. Unfortunately squatting in the house was not enough. No, though thousands of animals saw what took place, it was not enough. It is hard for me to say this, but I know that by this time next moon our defiance of the Great Lords will be forgotten, and,' Chu-lain's voice rose, 'the wrongs will continue. Yes, they will. For, friends,' he continued, 'we all know how the Great Lords are chosen and remain in their positions of power. Instead of each animal having one say by rights of jungle law, some animals have many says – animals friendly to the Great Lords . . . . '

He was interrupted by a young female flamingo who squawked a deep breath before asking, 'What do you mean, some animals have many says, Chu-lain? Soon I will be old enough to have my say. But I am only allowed one say by jungle law. Why do some animals have many says?'

Chu-lain smiled grimly, thought for a few seconds, then said, 'You know when it is time to have a say in electing the Great Lords all the animals old enough go to the giant cork tree to have their say. You know that each animal stands in front of the ancient cork and says, I give my say to . . . and he says the name of whatever animal he favours. The secretary birds record his say on bark-

paper. But when certain animals, certain Ru-clas animals
stand before the cork tree and say, I give my fifty says to
. . . and they say the name of the animal they favour, the
secretary birds also record their says, their fifty says. So
it is obvious who is elected.'

'But that's not fair,' screeched the flamingo.

'Exactly, my friend,' Chu-lain replied. 'It is not fair.
That is why I say it is time for all of us to take a stand. It
is time to demand one animal, one say. Then the choice of
Lords will be fair. Then maybe we can get laws passed to
allow us to live where we want to. After all, it is our right.
Our jungle right. It is time we marched to get our jungle
rights.'

All the animals grew very agitated at this.

Then an old rhinoceros growled, 'March? What do you
mean, Chu-lain?'

'Aye, Chu-lain,' squeaked a pink flamingo, fluttering
her wings in frustration. 'Tell us what you mean?'

'A march, that is exactly what I mean. A simple march
through the jungle to show the Great Lords and their
leader that we are all equal, that we should all have our
jungle rights. The right to choose where to live, the right
to choose our own Lords. We must march.'

'But who will go on this march, Chu-lain?' another fat-
jowled rhinoceros snorted, his face creasing into many
wrinkles.

'Why, you . . . and you . . . and you . . . ' shouted
Chu-lain pointing to Ru-clas and Lo-clas animals. 'All of
you and probably those who supported me at Cal-don.'

Now Tua-tal, his black eyes wild with excitement,
whispered, 'Do you really think the other animals will
march?'

Sighing, Chu-lain bowed his head and breathed loudly
for a few moments, then he whispered, 'I don't know,
Tua-tal. I really don't know. But can't you see, we have

to try.' Then looking out over the animals he shouted: 'Can't you all see that we have to march? We have to unite all the animals and the only way to do that is to have a peaceful march. We have to show the Great Lords that we will not put up with these wrongs any longer.'

At this, Emac, the old zebra, walked slowly over to Chu-lain – as he spoke his old grey head moved slowly up and down. 'I will march with you, Chu-lain. But I should warn you that we must be careful. The first thing we must do is tell Tigern-mas, the Leader of the Great Lords. Then the Law Leopards cannot say we are breaking jungle law.'

Chu-lain gaped at old Emac. 'Tell Tigern-mas? But for heaven's sake, why?'

'Aye, Emac. Why?' Tua-tal asked, his hairy eyebrows raised questioningly.

'Because it must be understood by every animal in Allegoria that we are having a peaceful march. They must be sure that we are not just out to make trouble, and we must be sure the Law Leopards will not attack us. Then, and only then, will we have the support from all, both Ru-clas and Lo-clas.'

Chu-lain and Tua-tal stared thoughtfully at the wise Emac.

Then Chu-lain shouted: 'Yes. I agree with you, Emac. We will do as you say. We will tell the Leader Tigern-mas of our plans for a peaceful march through Allegoria. We will march at noon, four days from now.'

'Aye . . . aye,' Tua-tal shouted, smiling at Chu-lain. 'Now let us decide how to control the marchers. We must have stewards to direct the crowds.'

'If providing there are crowds, Tua-tal,' Chu-lain said, but he began to get excited. 'Stewards, you say. Why I can think of no finer stewards than the rhinoceroses.' Rising on his hindlegs he beckoned to the huge beasts snorting in the muddy water, delighted with their role in the coming march.

'Who will tell Tigern-mas?' asked Tua-tal.

'Who else, but me,' Chu-lain said. 'I will make the journey tomorrow night. That will give us two days to get the march organised.'

'Ahem,' interrupted Emac. 'Maybe it would be better if I tell Tigern-mas.'

Chu-lain and Tua-tal stared at old Emac.

Then Tua-tal began to smile. 'Aye, Emac, maybe it would be better. Chu-lain here might insult the Great Leader and be thrown in the PIT.'

Now Chu-lain began to laugh and soon all the animals around the waterhole were laughing too.

An hour later, after many other details were discussed and it was decided that the march would start from Milesia, the meeting broke up. As old Emac made his way along the meandering paths to his house, his thoughts dwelt on the coming march. He whinnied nervously as he thought. If they did get support from both classes of animals then big changes would take place in jungle life. Big changes indeed. But excited as Emac was, he still felt a terrible dread. Somehow he sensed that if the march did take place then Allegoria would never be the same again.

4

Great Lord of Allegoria

One night later, Chu-lain and Tua-tal hurried to see Emac. The old white zebra was sitting by the waterhole at the centre of a group of pink flamingoes, answering their many questions. Away out in the water, a few rhinoceroses splashed lazily and a single crocodile, its two yellow eyes watchful antennaes, drifted towards a few bobbing ducks.

'But what if the Great Lord Tigern-mas doesn't allow the march, Emac?' a long-legged flamingo squawked. 'What do we do then?'

Slipping down along the bank, Chu-lain and Tua-tal sat down near the flamingoes.

Emac smiled at them then turned to the flamingo who had asked the last question. 'We can only hope that Tigern-mas will allow the march to take place. But rest assured, my feathered friends, I will be firm in putting my reasons for the march. I will make sure he understands that it will be a peaceful march. Yes, he will be reasonable, I know that.'

'He'll be reasonable, hah!' Chu-lain whispered angrily to Tua-tal. 'When was Tigern-mas ever reasonable?'

Chu-lain stared at old Emac, his nose twitching as a long blue dragonfly brushed past it. After more questions, Emac and two older flamingoes explained again why the march was so important.

As they listened, Chu-lain whispered to his zebra friend, 'What do you think, Tua-tal? Do you think Tigern-mas will forbid the march?'

Tua-tal's bright black eyes glistened with GUMPTION and he replied with a strange look on his face, 'I hope he doesn't allow the march to take place.' He whinnied with laughter at the surprised look on Chu-lain's face.

'You what?' Chu-lain spluttered.

'I said, I hope Tigern-mas forbids the march. And do you know why? Because if he doesn't allow the march, then twice as many will march.'

'Twice as many?' Chu-lain whispered, frowning. 'What do you mean?'

'Because,' Tua-tal said rolling over on one side to crush some angry soldier ants that were running on the dry stones beneath him, 'the Lo-clas, and even many of the Ru-clas have had enough of these wrongs. You saw how they flocked to Cal-don to support you. Not all mind you, but most of them. They need new leaders, Chu-lain. Leaders like yourself. Strong leaders. For Tigern-mas to forbid the march would be the last straw. They would get angry, and you know what angry animals are like, especially the younger ones.'

Slowly Chu-lain smiled as he began to understand what his friend had said. 'So you really think that Emac will not be able to persuade Tigern-mas?'

'Of course he won't. Oh, come on, Chu-lain. Think about it. Do you really believe Tigern-mas would allow anything that would threaten his leadership? He has to show the Great Lords that he is strong, that he will not bend to any class of animal. But let me add this, Chu-lain. If, or should I say when, Tigern-mas does forbid the march, the Law Leopards will come out in force. They will try to stop us.'

Then both zebra's attention was drawn to several pink flamingoes who were fluttering angrily into the air. With fierce flops they soon settled out near the edge of the waterhole. The angry words they squawked could be heard by everyone.

'We will not break jungle law if the march is forbidden.'

Old Emac whinnied softly, then his voice carried around the waterhole as he said, 'No one is asking you to break jungle law. The march has not been forbidden yet. I will persuade the Leader, Tigern-mas, that it will be a peaceful march. He will allow it, you'll see.'

Scowling the angry flamingoes kept silent, but other flamingoes began to shout at them.

One, a young, bow-legged creature with piercing eyes squawked, 'If you will not march, then be off with you. We don't need you. We have a chance to show every animal in the jungle that there must be no second-class animals. We will march whether it is allowed or not.'

All around him other young flamingoes nodded in agreement.

'See what I mean, Chu-lain,' whispered Tua-tal rising to his feet. 'Come on, let's give old Emac a paw.'

* * *

Later, as the three zebras trotted back to the main herd, Chu-lain said, 'Emac, you must go to Tigern-mas at Em-hain Castle tonight.'

Emac stopped and Tua-tal and Chu-lain stopped with him.

Snorting loudly Emac said, 'Yes, I have sent word with one of the pigeons, asking for an appointment. I will journey to Em-hain after dark.'

His two young friends were pleased by this.

As they galloped off again Emac said, 'I'm worried by Tigern-mas'. Then, after a pause he added: 'Ach, he'll see we are not looking for trouble. Aye, he'll allow the march alright.'

Winking slyly at Tua-tal, Chu-lain said, 'Yes, I think he will. But if he doesn't, no one will turn up.'

Now the two zebras smiled at each other as Emac suddenly stopped. Then he began to shake his grey head and paw at the ground.

'No one will turn up,' he whispered to himself. Then suddenly he looked at Chu-lain and Tua-tal and cried: 'But can't you see? Can't you see, Chu-lain? More animals will turn up if Tigern-mas forbids the march. Why didn't I think of it before? You know friends, I think my GUMPTION is beginning to fail.' He stared at the grinning Chu-lain and Tua-tal. 'You knew!' he shouted. 'You knew all along, didn't you? You knew more animals would march if the march was forbidden?' Now he began to smile too.

'Yes, Emac, we did,' Chu-lain said, nuzzling him affectionately.

Then Emac began to laugh heartily until he could hardly stand. Soon all three zebras were roaring with laughter.

Several parrots recorded all they had heard and seen that day.

Late that night Emac made his way through the dark and dangerous jungle ravine through Fann mountains. Eventually he came to a tall wooden gate and ahead in the moonlight stretched the long wide path that led to Em-hain Castle. As he stared through the gate which was slightly ajar, four Law Leopards sprang out from the bushes on each side of it.

'What are you doing here, old fool?' asked one of the leopards. 'Who gave you permission to come to

Em-hain?' He poked Emac in the nose with his longest claw.

The other three leopards grinned wickedly.

Emac shivered with fear as he faced the four growling leopards. Then he stammered? 'I . . . I . . . sent word with a pigeon earlier today. I have an appointment with the Great Lord Leader Tigern-mas. He is expecting me. I have come to ask permission for a peaceful march through Allegoria.'

'March!' another of the leopards snarled. Then he began to smile a slanted smile, wicked eyes glinting in the moonlight. 'We have heard of this. Let me tell you, foolish old zebra, we hope our Great Leader Tigern-mas allows the march.'

'Because,' roared the third leopard into Emac's frightened face, 'it will give us a chance to trample you Lo-clas, and any Ru-clas who are stupid enough to march with you. A march indeed! Who do you think you are, eh? Do you really believe our Great Leader will allow this? No chance of that, zebra. No chance.'

Then the fourth leopard whispered something.

The third leopard began to laugh. 'Ha, ha, ha, ha, ha. Go on you old fool,' he said, prodding Emac through the open gate. 'Go and see Tigern-mas. Waste your time, and if we see you anywhere near the march we will fix you, ha, ha, ha.'

Trembling with fear, Emac galloped towards Em-hain, a great wooden building six storeys tall with many rooms. It was built of thick barkless branches and it glittered eerily as Emac knocked on the door with his right front hoof. A few minutes later, after another couple of knocks, Tigern-mas's stout boar secretary opened the door and showed Emac into a great room.

Tigern-mas, a very fat, grotesque looking tiger with one eye, sprawled upon a mat made of coconut hair on a

dais at the far end of the room. He scowled as he opened his eye and saw the nervous zebra approach.

'Well?' he snapped.

Stuttering, Emac began: 'I . . . I . . . We have . . . '

'I know why you are here, zebra,' Tigern-mas roared. 'You think I don't know what goes on in Allegoria. Well let me tell you, Emac, I know everything about you and Chu-lain and the other troublemaker. I'll tell you right away, there's no way I will allow you to hold this march. I forbid it. In fact,' Tigern-mas snarled, rising quickly and crossing to a pile of thick bark parchments that lay in one corner of the great room. 'I have had this law drawn up.' He poked one of his sharp claws through the parchment and raised it up to his eye. 'It states that anyone who marches from Milesia will be thrown in the PIT for breaking jungle law . . . .'

The old white zebra's eyes grew wider, his fear left him and was replaced with anger. 'You forbid us to march, do you,' he shouted. 'Well let me tell you, the march will take place. We Lo-clas have had enough of your harsh jungle laws. We are all sick, sore and tired of your jungle wrongs. We will march. And do you know something, Tigern-mas? I will be proud to be at the head of the march.'

With an angry bellow, Tigern-mas leapt, landing on top of a now very scared Emac.

Tigern-mas's tail whipped angrily from side to side as he roared into Emac's face. 'You dare address me, me, like that. You dare defy me . . . ME, the greatest leader in all jungle history. You . . . you, the lowest of the low. Just because you have the GUMPTION does not make you any better in my eyes. I tell you, zebra, you are lucky you are old, or my anger would destroy you.'

Holding his noble white head erect, Emac faced the wicked leader and shouted: 'I do not fear you. You, or any of your Great Lords. Tomorrow I WILL march, and after . . . after, Allegoria will never be the same again. If you dare to stop us, you will be sorry. And for all time you will be blamed for starting the WHOLE HANDLIN': Aye . . . aye, Tigern-mas,' Emac shouted more loudly as he saw Tigern-mas's eyes widen. 'A WHOLE HANDLIN'.'

'A WHOLE HANDLIN',' roared Tigern-mas, after he had recovered from the shock. The patchy fur on the back of his neck stood straight out as he shouted, 'You are talking treason . . . TREASON, when you talk about a WHOLE HANDLIN' . . . Ahhh . . . get out . . . get out . . . get out before I forget how old you are. GET OUT.'

Backing towards the door, Emac heard the Great Lord Leader shout again: 'I have laid down the law, and if your animals or any Ru-clas march, I will have my Law Leopards cut you all down.'

From the door, Emac shouted back at Tigern-mas: 'The march will bring down Em-hain Castle. Aye, Tigern-mas, Em-hain. You and Em-hain will fall.'

These words had a strange effect upon the one-eyed tiger. Suddenly he was filled with fear.

Later as he hurried home, Emac shivered, then sighed. Now he could tell Chu-lain and Tua-tal they were right. The march had been forbidden. Now more animals would support them. The wheels of the WHOLE HANDLIN' had been set in motion.

And so the news spread throughout the jungle that Tigern-mas had banned the march, and like a fire out of control the animals grew angry, very angry. Many Lo-clas and Ru-clas clamoured to join the protest. An urgent meeting of the Allegoria Council was called by the three tiger lords.

The meeting was held in the great room at Em-hain Castle. A hundred and fifty Law Leopard Commanders and the Law Leopard Leader were there. The room was in an uproar when Tigern-mas padded quietly out onto the dais and sat down on his mat. He was angry with the great Tiger Lords of Allegoria and he trembled as he tried to keep himself under control. He glared at the three Tiger Lords who were arguing with some Law Leopard Commanders. Unable to control his anger anymore, Tigern-mas leapt to his feet.

'Quiet . . . all of you be quiet!' he roared, his sharp yellow teeth thick with saliva. 'Let us all conduct ourselves with dignity.' Then swinging to the Tiger Lords, he snarled: 'You three have called this meeting. Well, before you speak, let me tell you I am sick of your whining. SICK . . . SICK . . . SICK . . . DO YOU HEAR ME?'

Immediately every leopard in the room stopped breathing and turned to stare at the three terrified Tiger Lords.

'It's . . . it's just your decision we question, Leader. We three, we think you should allow this march to take place.'

'Oh,' growled Tigern-mas, moving across the dais towards the Tiger Lords, aware that several Commanders were nodding their heads in agreement with the Lord. 'You do, do you? Well then, tell me why?' He narrowed his eye as he glared at the fat Tiger Lords.

'Because, Leader,' another Tiger Lord said, 'because this march was forbidden, the Lo-clas zebras and others have got more support. Don't forget, some of our own class were always ready to march with them, but it's only since you banned it that many younger Ru-clas have decided to join them.'

Once again, Tigern-mas noted the nodding heads of more leopards. Then he spoke quickly. 'And tell me Lords. What if I change my mind now, eh? What then? Do you honestly think that that would satisfy Chu-lain and Emac, and that other troublemaker? Well, do you? No!' Tigern-mas suddenly roared, making the three Tiger Lords cower away from him. 'No, for they would want more. Now they want equal animalship, jungle rights, one animal, one say. Soon they will want our power. That is really what they are after. Can't you fools see that. They want a WHOLE HANDLIN'. They want to rule over us one day. Listen to me, all of you.' He paused for a moment, then went on, his voice dropping as he stepped away from the Tiger Lords, 'they must not march. You leopards will stop them, and beat them down. Give them a trouncing they will never forget. Beat them, and I know . . . I know you will hear no more of marches after that. Ten battalions of the strongest Law Leopards will be enough. And we do have the elephants.' Smiling now, he saw that every leopard in the room was nodding in agreement. 'Well then, what do you think now? Do you still believe I should allow the march to take place?'

Shuffling towards him, one of the Tiger Lords began to speak. 'We think . . . '

Suddenly he was interrupted by the Law Leopard Leader who shouted: 'We will stop them. We will finish all this, Great Leader. Leave everything to us. We will stop the march.'

'Aye . . . aye . . . ' roared every leopard in the room. Tigern-mas looked at the Tiger Lords. They stared steadily at him and all three nodded.

Later, as Tigern-mas watched the leopards and the Tiger Lords leave the great room, he pondered. At the back of his mind he felt somehow he had made the wrong decision. With a loud sigh, he rose from the mat and leaped down from the dais onto the floor, crossed it and went into a smaller room. Quickly he poured himself a coconutshell of jungle juice and gulped it down. Then he

refilled the shell again.

Later that night a Giraffe Lord called Cu-roi, and a Leopard Commander secretly met near a group of high rubber trees.

'You say you will be out in force tomorrow to stop the marchers,' whispered Cu-roi.

'Yes, your Lordship. We are to stop the march just outside Milesia. We are to teach these troublemakers a lesson. We are to beat them.'

'Beat them,' Cu-roi said thoughtfully. 'A great mistake.'

'A mistake?' the commander said, frowning.

'Yes,' Cu-roi answered. Then he quickly thanked the commander for the information and they parted. Later as he loped home he shivered excitedly. Yes, a great mistake, he thought. Soon I will be able to make my move to replace Tigern-mas as Great Leader. When I am Leader I will give the Lo-clas animal one say. That is their jungle right. I will be a just Leader, respected by Lo-clas and Ru-clas. Yes, soon . . . soon.

5

A First Blow

At fifteen minutes before noon on the day of the march, Chu-lain, Tua-tal and Emac visited by the grove of mahogany trees in Milesia. They could see that only about one hundred of the smallest animals had turned up, Lo-clas and Ru-clas, including a rat, frogs, mice, ant-eaters, two beautiful monkeys, a doe and five armadillos. There were twelve rhinoceros stewards there too. In the midst of a tiny group of monkeys, Chu-lain saw Ja-no, Mo-li and their family.

'There aren't many, Tua-tal,' Chu-lain whispered, his ears pointing straight up with anxiety. He was also listening for any sound of movement from the trees, where he could see several parakeets and some parrots and a few other unusual and colourful birds.

'Ach, Chu-lain,' Tua-tal said, 'give them a little more time. We've a few minutes left.'

Just in front of them, old Emac, his head held proudly erect, stood ready. He didn't care how many marchers there were, for this was the time he had dreamed about all his life. Now, he thought, after we have defied the Great Leader Tigern-mas, all the animals in Allegoria will understand why we marched. How important it is.

At two minutes to noon, Chu-lain's ears pricked up even higher, and then they all saw them. Coming through the trees, hundreds of animals, monkeys, deer, antelope, flamingoes, buffaloes, zebras, ibex, cheetahs, panthers, snakes, and many other types and of both classes. Some of the monkeys carried banners made from broad leaves which read 'ONE ANIMAL, ONE SAY'. Other monkeys had banners which read 'END WRONGS NOW', and 'BETTER HOUSES FOR ALL'. Two huge buffaloes carried a banner which read 'EQUAL RIGHTS FOR EVERY ANIMAL'.

With tears in his eyes, Chu-lain looked at his friends. Old Emac sniffed and Tua-tal whinnied excited greetings.

At twelve o'clock Chu-lain stood on his hindlegs and spoke to all the animals. 'First of all, I want to make it clear to every animal here that this march has been banned by Tigern-mas. We will be breaking jungle law. But by marching we will make all the animals in Allegoria realise that we must be equal. Lo-clas and Ru-clas, equal. Once again, if any of you have doubts, don't take part. If you march, you will be breaking jungle law.'

'The law is broken every day by the leopards,' a huge Lo-clas rhinoceros bellowed, his great gaping mouth opening wider.

'Aye,' a beautiful Ru-clas doe squealed. 'We all must be treated the same. We are all equal.'

'And that is why both Ru-clas and Lo-clas are here today. They know we are all equal. They see that there is much wrong in our jungle,' shouted Chu-lain.

Then Tua-tal began to speak and the flies buzzed around the many sun-baked animals as they listened to his words. 'We will shortly be moving into the trees and onto the paths. We know the Law Leopards will be waiting to stop us. We are going to confront them, PEACEFULLY. I say PEACEFULLY, for this is a PEACEFUL march. Hopefully the Law Leopards will see reason and allow us to go on with our peaceful march. If they try to stop us, I fear there will be trouble, but we will have to try and move through them.'

At this Chu-lain smiled. Aye, he thought, the Law Leopards will have to use force to stop us.

'Well then,' shouted Tua-tal. 'Are you ready? Are we all ready?'

'Aye . . . aye we're ready,' shouted all the animals in unison.

'Are you ready to make jungle history?'

'Aye . . . aye . . . aye . . . ' the hysterical animals screamed.

'Then come on. Let the march begin. Follow Emac, Chu-lain and myself.'

Snorting, the three zebras moved towards the trees together and after them the excited marchers. Some of them began to sing.

'WE SHALL ALL BE E . . . EQUAL. WE SHALL ALL BE E . . . EQUAL. WE SHALL ALL BE EQUAL SOME DAY . . AY . . . AY . . . AY . . . AY. FO . . . OR DEEP IN OUR HEARTS, WE DO BELIEVE, WE SHALL ALL BE EQUAL SOME DAY.'

The sleek Law Leopards heard the singing and grinned. All along the wide path they stood, swinging heavy mahogany batons and wearing helmets made from half coconut shells. Some carried protective shields made from the skins of dead animals. Behind the five hundred law Leopards stood forty of the biggest elephants in the jungle, foul water dripping from their long swinging trunks.

'WE SHALL ALL BE E . . . EQUAL. WE SHALL ALL BE EQUAL . . . '

Then the marchers came into view and the leopards stiffened, snarling. They were without fear and their spotted tails stood straight out behind them.

Without fear too, Chu-lain, Tua-tal, and Emac led the singing marchers right up to the leopard barrier. Rising on his hindlegs, Chu-lain turned and signalled for all the marchers to stop.

Then, just as he landed back on all fours again, the leader of the Law Leopards stepped towards him. Raising a megaphone made from beeswax in his front paws, he roared into it. 'THIS MARCH HAS BEEN FORBIDDEN BY OUR GREAT LEADER TIGERN-MAS. YOU ARE ALL BREAKING JUNGLE LAW. IF YOU DO NOT DISPERSE AND GO HOME MY LAW LEOPARDS WILL ARREST YOUR LEADERS. YOU HAVE ONE MINUTE TO MAKE UP YOUR MINDS.' Lowering the megaphone he stared past Chu-lain and his two zebra comrades. He could see the uncertainty of some of the marchers' faces.

An uneasy silence fell.

Noticing this, Chu-lain shouted: 'Do not forget why we are here. Our rights. Our equal rights. They will not stop us. We march for all animals in the jungle . . . .'

'YOU HAVE THIRTY SECONDS,' the leader of the Law Leopards roared through his megaphone. Tua-tal pushed forward. 'Are you going to attack us, eh? Ahhhh!'

A Law Leopard had suddenly raised his baton and clubbed Tua-tal on the side of his head. Then two other Law Leopards attacked Emac and the old zebra fell to the ground, blood pumping from his head. Advancing and whacking their batons, the leopards now moved into the marchers. Chu-lain cursed as he saw a young doe fall on her side under a barrage of fierce blows from a frenzied leopard. Then the elephants began to plough into the marchers. Terrified, the smaller animals ran aimlessly around, squealing with fear as they were hit by blasts of foul water from the elephants' trunks. The monkeys took to the trees and began to fight back. Snapping off sticks, they threw them at the leopards, and some hurled their banners down onto a group of angry spitting leopards.

The din of the rioting grew louder and carried through the jungle.

Parrots, safe in the trees, recorded all that was happening.

Hours later, when peace was restored, news of the riot had reached all four corners of the jungle and beyond. The news was carried even to Lionia, far across the wide water.

That night, although still suffering from a sore head, old Emac felt happy. He knew that what had happened would be told and retold by every animal in the jungle. He smiled as he listened to his young companions.

'The parrots will carry the truth about what happened today,' Chu-lain said. 'Those Law Leopards will be sorry for all the pain they inflicted on us.'

*   *   *

Meanwhile at the other end of Allegoria, in Em-hain Castle, Tigern-mas spoke with several high-ranking officers and their leader about the day's events. He was pleased with the way everything had turned out.

'Officers,' he said, smiling, 'you and your leopards have done well this day. You all deserve the greatest praise for the way you did your jungle duty. You beat the troublemakers. They will never try to march again. They have learned a lesson they will never forget.'

'Aye . . . one animal, one say . . . Ha, ha, ha, ha,' laughed the leader of the Law Leopards. 'We gave them one animal, one say alright. Ha, ha, ha, ha, ha. A lot of good their GUMPTION was today. Ha, ha, ha, ha, ha.'

Tigern-mas smiled again as he listened to the officers gloat. Aye, he thought, there will be no more talk of marches after this.

But he was wrong. Very wrong.

6

The Long March

Not many moons later Tigern-mas was awakened from his afternoon sleep.

He cursed, stretching himself, the loose striped folds of his body rolling out like a barber's pole. 'What is it?' His extended claws tore at the coconut mat. 'Why have you wakened me?' Jumping to his feet, he took a long curving swipe at his secretary.

The sow boar dodged away just in time. 'Sssorry, your leadership,' she stammered. 'It's . . . it's another march . . .'

Tigern-mas glared at her. 'A what? A march? What march? Not those zebras again?'

'No, no, your leadership,' the boar said, moving closer. 'It's not the zebras. New organisers. Pigeons have been sent by them to ask permission for the march. Right across the jungle they say. From Nemedia, all the way to Milesia, where the first march started.'

Tigern-mas rubbed the sleep from his eyes as he snarled, 'So they have sent the pigeons, have they? Send for the Great Lords. I want them, and all the Law Leopard Officers. I also want all the information you can get on these new organisers. I'll warrant you those accursed zebras are behind this . . . WELL, why are you standing there? Send for the Lords. Get my Law Officers here . . . HURRY . . . HURRY . . . .'

The boar secretary ran from the room and along a narrow corridor. Seconds later she stood on the front porch of Em-hain. Two sleeping pelicans were rudely awakened as the excited boar related Tigern-mas's message.

Inside, Tigern-mas pondered on this new occurrence. Another damned march. This time I will force the Lords to take the decision, he vowed.

* * *

The Law Officers were demanding that Tigern-mas forbid the march. Then the Tiger Lords swept into the meeting with the biggest Gorilla Lord in the jungle. His name was Ath-ach. He stood over two metres tall. A white streak of hair grew from a point between his black beady eyes, stretched down the back of his head and around his bulging muscled neck. Tigern-mas smiled affectionately at him. It is good to see my old friend again, he thought, he'll back me up.

Then one of the Tiger Lords roared: 'Forbidding the last march was a mistake, leader. You know that. You all know that,' he added, looking around at the leopards. Turning back to Tigern-mas he shouted: 'This time you must allow the march.'

For a moment there was silence and every animal looked at Tigern-mas.

Ath-ach studied Tigern-mas's inscrutable face. Then he swayed towards the dais and turning towards the Tiger Lords roared in a voice that shook the whole building: 'I agree. The march must take place.'

The three Tiger Lords and Tigern-mas stared at Ath-ach in amazement as he spoke on.

'Let me tell you this,' he boomed, thumping his black chest. 'If these marchers try to march from Nemedia to

Milesia they will see that not all Ru-clas are fools. No, our kind will not allow them through their part of the jungle. Our own Ru-clas must believe we are giving in to these troublemakers. Then they will decide what to do. Ru-clas will stop them.' He glared around the room. All the leopard officers were nodding in agreement. Then he turned to Tigern-mas and said quietly, 'Sign the order, Tigern-mas. Allow the march.'

Tigern-mas stared at him, nodded to the Tiger Lords, then rapped his tail on a hollow log behind him. He waited until his secretary came running in. 'Draw up a proclamation. State on it that I will allow this march. I will sign it.'

'Eh?' his boar secretary stared.

'You heard me,' roared Tigern-mas. 'Do it!'

Her eyes wide with fear, the sow boar ran from the room.

Later, after the Tiger Lords and the Law Leopards had gone, Ath-ach sat on the mat beside Tigern-mas.

'Ach,' boomed Ath-ach, 'the leopards will do as we tell them. They are loyal to their own. They will always back us up. You have nothing to worry about. The marchers will learn that the journey from Nemedia to Milesia will be a long hard one. That is,' Ath-ach smiled, rubbing his hairy chin with his stubby right forefinger, 'if they ever reach Milesia.'

Tigern-mas stared at him. 'You have a plan?'

'Not yet, but my friend Mug-nu will not be long in drawing one up. You know Mug-nu, he will think of something.'

With a long sigh Tigern-mas scrambled to his feet and began pacing up and down.

Ath-ach studied him for a few moments. 'Tell me, Tigern-mas,' he asked, 'how have you been keeping? You don't look at all like the tiger I knew. Your fur is not as shiny as it used to be either, and you have lost a lot of weight. I can almost see your ribs.'

Tigern-mas stopped, then sat down beside his friend again. He looked at him. 'It's these dreams, Ath-ach.'

'Dreams?'

'Aye, dreams, horrible dreams. They started on the day of the first march.' He shivered.

Ath-ach reached out and put a paw on Tigern-mas's bony shoulder and whispered softly, 'Tell me about the dreams.'

'I dream . . . this dream. It's the same dream every night. I dream all the animals in the jungle are equal. The Lo-clas even have better houses than the Ru-clas. It . . . it's horrible.' He shuddered again. 'And do you know the worst part . . . the Lo-clas . . . the Lo-clas are allowed one animal, one say.' He was silent for a while. 'Last night I woke up screaming. I couldn't get to sleep for a long time after.'

Ath-ach's fierce face softened, and patting Tigern-mas on the head, he said, 'Sure it's only a dream. You know it is. You know that can never happen. We would never allow it. Ach, Tigern-mas, this march is a last attempt to seize power. Can't you see that? Soon the jungle will again be the way it always was.'

'I hope you're right, Ath-ach,' Tigern-mas whispered.

'You know I am.' Ath-ach smiled and stood up. 'Well now, I must be off. I'll drop by later to see how you are. Don't worry, Tigern-mas, soon it will all be over. You'll see.'

Tigern-mas watched his friend amble across the floor of the great hall. Then as Ath-ach closed the door behind him, Tigern-mas rose and hurried to another room. There he stared at the container of jungle juice, and reached out to pour a little of it into a coconut cup.

* * *

At their secret meeting-place, Cu-roi and the Law Leopard officer discussed Tigern-mas allowing the march.

'So Ath-ach has involved himself now,' Cu-roi said. 'And he thinks that this is a last attempt by the Lo-clas to seize power. Well he is wrong.'

'Is he?' the Law Leopard officer asked, frowning.

'Yes,' Cu-roi said, looking down at him, his long neck stretching higher. 'Perhaps now all this will work out to my advantage.' Then he stared steadily at the officer. 'When I make my move to unseat Tigern-mas I'll expect you to support me.'

'You know I will,' the leopard snarled. 'You promised me the Law Leopard Leadership when you are Leader.'

'Yes,' Cu-roi said smiling. 'I did, didn't I.'

They smiled at each other.

*   *   *

On the first day of the following year, twenty monkeys, ten giraffes, four deer, twelve rhinoceros, fourteen antelopes, eighteen ostriches and two sleek jaguars set out from Nemedia. The jaguars were called Con-lai and Con-ran and they had organised this march, for they had seen what Chu-lain and his zebra friends had tried to do. Sometimes they called themselves the Juggernaut Jaguars.

From the first second the marchers were attacked. They were punched, spat upon and had terrible insults shouted at them by several small groups of Ru-clas. The brave marchers took it all without retaliating, and they marched on. High in the trees the exotic hummingbirds and multicoloured parrots watched their slow progress and spread the news of what was happening.

More animals joined when they heard the news, and on the second day about one thousand were marching. Still they were attacked, and still they refused to retaliate.

With just one day of walking to go to reach Milesia, the marchers rested at a place called Mara.

*   *   *

'I never thought they would get this far,' roared Mug-nu. 'We have to stop them, Ath-ach, and I have just the plan. But I will need your help, and help from your kind.'

'The Gorillas?' Ath-ach asked, studying Mug-nu, a stout black-faced leader of the Avatar Apes.

'Aye. Don't tell me you thought I was going to allow these troublemakers to reach Milesia unscathed?'

'Well, no,' Ath-ach growled. 'I guessed you would have some plan.'

'And I have,' Mug-nu said, twirling a short baton around twice and tucking it expertly under his hairy armpit. Then he explained his terrible plan to Ath-ach.

*   *   *

That same night at a secret meeting in a great room in the biggest house in Milesia, Mug-nu and Ath-ach addressed one thousand fierce gorillas.

Mug-nu, who was a persuasive speaker, raised his arm and roared out, 'These marchers, these troublemakers, for that's what they are, these troublemakers pretend they are marching for equal jungle rights. But we all know what they are really marching for. They and their Juggernaut Jaguars believe they can pull the fur over our eyes. But no . . . no, we are not as stupid as they think we are. No, my friend, this march is a sham. Aye, a lie. They are a threat to our way of life. If they are allowed to reach Milesia they will have won a victory. They will have got what they wanted . . . and what is it they want? eh? Why, nothing less than one animal, one say. They want to rule US. They believe they are better than us! Well, my friends, are we really going to allow these evil animals to reach Milesia? Are we? Are we going to allow them to march triumphantly into Milesia and brag to their own how they made fools of us? Well, are we? Are we?'

'Noooo . . . Nooooo,' screamed some of the younger gorillas, thumping their chests loudly. Other gorillas, who carried clubs with sharp thorns sticking out of them, scowled and picked their noses.

'Aye, that's right,' Mug-nu continued. 'They will be stopped. They will be stopped, and given a dose of medicine they will never forget. Listen to me, all of you. These evil Jaguars and their followers have to be stopped before this disease spreads throughout the rest of our great jungle.'

'It will be stopped,' roared Ath-ach, stepping beside Mug-nu. He glared down at the tribe of gorillas. 'Well, what do you say? Are you all with us?'

'Aye . . . aye, we're with you, Ath-ach. You and Mug-nu. We will destroy these evil troublemakers,' roared a huge gorilla, his face almost purple with hate.

As the room erupted with loud roars from the gorillas, Mug-nu smiled at Ath-ach. Then he held up his paw and shouted: 'Listen to me, all of you. I have a plan. A plan to defeat our enemies. But I need your help.' He paused, waiting for the expected reply.

'Tell us what you want, Mug-nu. We are loyal to you and Ath-ach. Tell us what to do,' roared a heavy-set gorilla holding up a thick black wooden club.

'Aye . . . aye, lead us Mug-nu. Lead us. We will follow you,' shouted another gorilla.

Once again, as the room resounded with roars, Mug-nu smiled at Ath-ach. Then he shouted: 'Very well then. Here is what I want you to do . . . .'

*   *   *

Outside, hiding in the shadows under a group of banana trees, a stout, dark-striped zebra called Bu-inn and his companion Tua-tal watched as the gorillas came bellowing out of the house and crashed away along the paths leading out of Milesia.

'That Mug-nu and Ath-ach are up to no good,' Tua-tal whispered.

'Look out,' warned Bu-inn. 'Here they come.'

Holding their breaths, the two zebras stared as Ath-ach and Mug-nu emerged from the house. With smiles on their faces they shook paws. Suddenly, Ath-ach began to sniff the air. Then his tiny ears pricked up and the white hair on his head stood straight up. With a roar he turned and, narrowing his beady eyes he stared straight at the spot where the two zebras were hiding. Seeing they had been discovered, Bu-inn and Tua-tal stepped out into the moonlight. Recognising them, Mug-nu growled and beat his chest.

Then Ath-ach said, 'Two more would-be marchers. Come on Mug-nu. Let us get home, the smell here is foul.'

As they walked away, growling with laughter, Bu-inn grew very angry and shouted after them: 'Tomorrow Milesia will be finished with the likes of you. Tomorrow your power over the Lo-clas will be over. When the marchers reach Milesia they will receive a welcome that will be so tremendous it will be heard throughout the jungle. Every animal, and I do mean *every* animal, Ru-clas and Lo-clas will know that the days of the jungle lords are numbered.'

With an angry roar Ath-ach turned, his beady eyes glaring with hatred at Bu-inn: 'Numbered,' he snarled. 'No, power will always be in the paws of the Ru-clas

Lords. As for the marchers, perhaps,' he spat, 'perhaps the marchers won't reach Milesia.'

With a quick whisper Mug-nu pulled him on. With a sneering grin at Bu-inn, Ath-ach and Mug-nu ambled away into the trees. Soon Tua-tal and Bu-inn could hear their laughter in the distance.

'They're definitely up to something, Tua-tal,' Bu-inn said. 'And I've a feeling we'll know all about it tomorrow,' he added ominously.

7

Ambush at Fay-Linn

It was a cold morning. Con-lai and Con-ran, the Juggernaut Jaguars, led two hundred and fifty marchers out of Mara and into the high, tree-covered mountains. Over seven hundred other animals, including the heavy, short-legged rhinoceroses had fallen behind. As they marched along the paths they knew they were being watched by many Law Leopards.

At mid-day they descended into Fay-Linn, a long, narrow valley, bordered on both sides by low ditches and high trees. As they came down the winding path Con-lai sensed something was wrong. Raising his head he sniffed into the wind. He listened. Then he looked up into the trees on each side of him. Why aren't the birds singing, he thought. But then his sharp hearing picked up a slight rustling of leaves.

'I don't like this, Con-ran,' he whispered to his jaguar comrade. 'We are being watched, and not by the law leopards.'

Con-ran stared up into the trees, but he could see nothing unusual.

Suddenly a young female gorilla dropped from a branch above them. She landed on all fours at their paws. Then she straightened and, standing with her legs apart, beat violently on her chest, screaming in a high-pitched voice, her sharp teeth glistening in the sun: 'Ath-ach . . .

Ath-ach . . . Ath-ach.'

'Look to yourselves,' screamed Con-lai, the hairs on the back of his neck standing straight up with fear.

The ambush had begun.

From high in the trees the marchers heard the sounds of breaking branches as the gorillas and apes dropped closer to their prey. Stones and sticks rained down on the terrified marchers. Then several huge Avatar Apes led by Mug-nu dropped almost beside Con-lai and Con-ran and wielding heavy clubs, tore into the two jaguars.

'Run, protect yourself, Con-ran,' shouted Con-lai just before he was clubbed to the ground.

Con-ran gasped, horrified, as he stared for a moment at his injured friend. Ignoring his own attackers, he licked Con-lai's face. Then a blow from a gorilla's club knocked him sideways. The breath rushed from his body. He was hit again and again. Battered almost unconscious, he dived for the undergrowth, seeking cover. As he did so, he heard cries of pain and terror from other marchers as they were attacked.

'Beat them . . . beat them senseless,' Con-ran heard the voice of Mug-nu scream. 'Teach them that we Ru-clas are the chosen animals. Beat them . . . Don't let them rise again. Teach them a lesson they will never forget . . . BEAT THEM . . . . '

❧　❧　❧

An hour later the marchers had been scattered all over the valley. Many of them were badly injured. Tired and triumphant, the gorillas and the apes ambled away. Crawling painfully from his hiding-place, Con-ran searched for Con-lai. He found the jaguar lying by the side of the path. A female monkey, blood trickling from wounds on her tail, was helping him. At least he is still alive, Con-ran thought, as he crawled towards them.

Later still, when the marchers had gathered together again, Con-ran listened to some monkeys that had been badly beaten.

Chattering angrily, one gibbon screeched, 'I saw the Law Leopards away up in the trees. They were watching everything and they didn't try to help us.'

'Aye,' a lemur cried, 'they just stood in the trees laughing with the gorillas . . . I saw them . . . I did.'

'So much for the law of the jungle,' Con-ran hissed to himself.

An hour later, the exhausted and injured marchers reached Milesia, where thousands of Lo-clas and many Ru-clas who had heard about what had happened and were very ashamed and angry with Mug-nu, were waiting to give them a hero's welcome. Earlier the parrots had carried the terrible news of the ambush to the animals in Milesia. Slowly the marchers moved through the crowds of cheering animals and on into a great clearing in the middle of Milesia, where Tua-tal, Bu-inn and the other zebras were waiting to welcome them.

*   *   *

The news of the joyous welcome for the marchers soon reached Tigern-mas and that night, seething with anger, he gave secret orders to two Leopard Officers.

Throughout the time of darkness, these officers and one hundred Law Leopards terrorised the animals living in a part of Milesia called the Swamplands. Dragging out several antelope and one old rhinoceros, they subjected them to abuse and ridicule. Laughing and jeering they lashed out at some female monkeys who had just happened to be swinging by. An old zebra called Sa-de, who was very ill, was beaten by some leopards who broke into his house and dragged him from his sick bed. Awakened by the disturbance, more and more animals in the Swamplands came out to see what was going on. They too suffered the same abuse as the others.

* * *

Early the next morning, Bu-inn and Tua-tal made the journey to the Law Leopards' headquarters. They demanded to see the officer leopard in charge. It was some time before he came out to see them, but when Bu-inn and Tua-tal angrily told him about the disgraceful conduct of the Law Leopards in the Swamplands the night before, he smiled. His smile turned to a sneer, and then a scowl as he grew angry.

Bu-inn shouted: 'This attack on the animals of the Swamplands has been recorded by the hummingbirds. We demand a promise from you and Tigern-mas that it will not happen again. The Law Leopards will never again enter the Swamplands unless there are riots there.'

With a loud roar, unable to contain his anger any longer, the leopard officer sprang to his feet saying: 'And just who do you think you are, giving orders to me? Listen, zebra, we are the law, and we can go anywhere in the jungle.'

Even angrier now, Bu-inn screamed back: 'You will never enter the Swamplands. You and your Law Leopards have shown the Swamplanders what you are really like. Last night you terrified many of them. It will never happen again . . . NEVER.'

'Oh, will it not?' roared the officer right into Bu-inn's face. 'Well, I'll tell you, and the rest of you hateful Lo-clas, we Law Leopards can do whatever we please. We have the power. You have a nerve to think that you are equal to us. Do you really believe that stupid march will make any difference? Well, do you? If you do, you are far mistaken.'

'No,' Bu-inn said, calming down. 'It is you who is mistaken. Already, because of the fear you caused last night, the animals in the Swamplands are building a barrier to keep you out. So,' Bu-inn added, then paused a moment, pleased at the shocked expression on the leopard officer's face, 'you will not enter the Swamplands again. Never.'

With a loud snarl the leopard officer turned to four white cockatoos sitting on the branch behind him. 'Report every word that has been said here to leader Tigern-mas. Make sure he hears about this barrier.' As the cockatoos flew off, the officer turned back to Bu-inn and Tua-tal. 'Now, we will see who runs the jungle. Now you and the rest of you Lo-clas will learn what it means to defy us. Tonight all this will end. Tonight that barrier will be torn down and the animals in the Swamplands punished.' With a final glare at the two zebras he turned and slipped out the door to prepare his Law Leopards.

As the two zebras galloped back to the Swamplands, Tua-tal said: 'This is really the beginning, Bu-inn. Chu-lain will be pleased.'

'Aye,' Bu-inn replied grimly. 'He will. Soon word will reach even to Lionia. The lions will have to interfere.'

'Do you really think they will?'

'Aye, Tua-tal, I do. They'll have to. There will be a battle at the Swamplands. It is there Allegoria's future will be decided.'

At the entrance to the Swamplands they had to jump over a part of the barrier that had already been erected. Inside, they could see the huge piles of stones and sharp sticks that had been gathered by hundreds of young monkeys. Older monkeys and other animals were making the barrier stronger by intertwining thick branches. It will have to be very strong, thought Bu-inn, to keep the elephants out. Then he saw the part of the barrier he and Tua-tal had just jumped over, getting branched up. The Swamplanders were safe, but they were also trapped.

* * *

When Tigern-mas heard about the barrier he immediately called a meeting of all the Law Leopard officers. Ath-ach, the Tiger Lords and several other high-ranking lords were present in the great hall at Em-hain. Cu-roi was there. As he passed Ath-ach he glared at him. Ath-ach bared his yellow teeth at Cu-roi and thumped his chest angrily. Every animal there knew there was no love lost between the Gorilla Lord and the Giraffe Lord

Cu-roi. The reason for this had mainly to do with Ath-ach, for he suspected that Cu-roi favoured one animal, one say.

'One thing is certain,' a Tiger Lord shouted as the reason for the meeting was made clear. 'We cannot allow the Lo-clas in the Swamplands to have a barrier. There can be no barriers in Allegoria. There can be no FORBIDDEN places. This time the Lo-clas have overstepped themselves.'

'Aye,' another Tiger Lord roared, interrupting his comrade. 'Now is the time to trample them down. Now is the time to destroy them.'

'Destroy them,' growled a third Tiger Lord. 'And squash this barrier now.'

Tigern-mas looked around the packed room. Steam rose from all the angry animals' bodies as they hotly debated the issue. He thought, it's all Ath-ach's fault anyway. The Lo-clas are angry with him. They're angry at Mug-nu too for attacking the marchers. They'll never be cowed now.

'What are we going to do then?' roared one of the Tiger Lords.

Suddenly Ath-ach, his eyes bulging and growing redder with every breath, roared: 'I'll tell you what you are going to do. You'll order ten full battalions of Law Leopards down into the Swamplands. They will rout out the Lo-class leaders. Take the elephants, smash the barrier and drag out the zebras and the jaguars. Throw them in the PIT forever. Then you will have no more trouble. Drag them out, I say. Aye, drag them out!'

'But,' a fat leopard officer growled, 'there are probably a few thousand Lo-clas in the Swamplands. They will be prepared.'

'Then take a hundred battalions. Take as many as you need. Call up the H-hyenas. They've been idle for too long,' Ath-ach roared. 'But do it quickly. We don't want word of this to reach the Lions in Lionia. We don't want them to think we can't run our own jungle.' He glared around the room, his chest heaving.

Then Tigern-mas spoke. He looked nervous and his voice was low and hoarse. 'The Lions have heard already. They will want to see how we handle this. If we can't handle it, they will interfere.'

'They won't have to,' roared Ath-ach, his eyes redder than before. 'We will handle it.' Then he began to beat his chest again, roaring, 'Squash the Lo-clas into the Swamplands. Do it now. Today. Catch them on the hop. They won't be expecting us so soon. The longer this goes on the more the Lions of Lionia WILL think we can't run Allegoria.'

Tigern-mas sighed silently, then looked at the Tiger Lords. They nodded to him. He turned and looked around the room at the leopards. They too nodded. Then he looked at Ath-ach, who growled deep and nodded as well.

Then Cu-roi, the Giraffe Lord made his move. 'Listen to me, all of you. Why should there have to be trouble? Why should we attack the Swamplands? All this will end if the Lo-clas are given one animal, one say. That is all they want. Give it to them and all this will be forgotten . . .'

'Nooooo,' roared Ath-ach, making every leopard jump. 'They are not like us. They do not think like us. They can't have the same as us. Why should there be one animal, one say . . . Soon they would rule over us. Besides, it's too late for that, much too late. They have broken jungle law. They must be punished.'

'No,' shouted Cu-roi, stretching his graceful neck, 'it's not too late. I say give them one animal, one say, and better houses. They do NOT want to rule.'

Ath-ach glared at Cu-roi as the leopards began to argue amongst themselves again. They were now unsure what to do.

'So it will all end if we give them one animal, one say, and promises, will it now?' Ath-ach snarled. 'No, I don't think so.' He turned to face the leopards as he shouted: 'Listen to me. If the Lo-clas get away with this.. . . this defiance of jungle law . . . if we allow them one animal, one say, and better housing and whatever else they want, they will think we are weak. Then they will demand more, and MORE and MORE, until finally they . . . AYE, they will want control of all Allegoria. They will control US. Tell me, do you want that? WELL, DO YOU?'

'NOOOOOO . . . NOOOOOO,' screamed the angry leopards.

'Let us destroy them, Tigern-mas,' roared the Leopard Leader. 'Let us crush them. Let us tear down this barrier and crush them . . . .'

'YESSSS . . . YESSSS,' screamed his officers.

With a smile on his face, Ath-ach looked up at Tigern-mas, who was staring at Cu-roi. Cu-roi was shaking his head. Now all the leopards looked at a grim-faced Tigern-mas. With his long tongue he licked his dry lips slowly, then whispered, 'Do it.'

'HURRAYYYY . . . HURRAYYY,' cheered the leopards.

A few seconds later, they slinked away from the great hall. Ath-ach, Tigern-mas, the Tiger Lords, Cu-roi the Giraffe Lord and a few other lords remained.

'Tigern-mas,' Cu-roi said quietly. 'Can't you see that you are making a terrible mistake?'

'The only mistake that's been made,' snarled Ath-ach is letting spineless giraffes like you into our council.'

Swinging his neck slowly, Cu-roi said to Ath-ach,

'Can't you see that your bully tactics won't work this time. The Lo-clas won't cow down now. They've had enough. They'll fight. They are our equals, we should accept that.'

'Accept . . . accept them,' roared Ath-ach, the white hair on his neck bristling. 'Never. They are not our equals. They are Lo-clas. We are the chosen animals. We have been chosen to run Allegoria the way we see fit. This right has been handed down to us by our fathers and our forefathers. No one will ever take that right away from us.'

Cu-roi sighed again, then turned to the rest of the lords, saying: 'If this turns out badly, I challenge Tigern-mas to step down as leader. Then I ask the Council to accept me as leader in his place.'

All the lords stared at him. Then they looked at Tigern-mas.

'Accept . . . accept,' roared Ath-ach to Tigern-mas. 'Tomorrow it will all be over. Tomorrow peace will be restored to Allegoria and your leadership will be unchallenged . . . ACCEPT.'

Now everyone looked at Tigern-mas.

'Very well,' he said shakily. 'If this turns out badly I will resign. I will be glad to hand over to you, Cu-roi. Now please . . . please excuse me. This meeting is over . . . .'

The others watched him as slowly he left the great hall. With a final glare at Cu-roi, Ath-ach left too, followed by the three Tiger Lords.

In his own room, Tigern-mas trembled as he poured himself a half coconut cup of jungle juice. He drank it all down quickly then poured himself another.

8

Barricade of the Swamplands

The Swamplands were sinking, dark islands of reed on a stagnant, treacherous marsh in the centre of Milesia. Most of the houses, though built on stilts were damp and in bad repair. All around the edge of the marsh poisoned gases rose continuously. Any animal who inhaled these putrid gases died instantly. There was only one safe entrance to the Swamplands and now this was completely sealed by a barrier, which was twenty metres wide and fifteen metres high. Hundreds of monkeys swarmed all over it. Many of them sat on top of it, chattering excitedly, waiting, waiting, for the leopards to come.

'THE LAW LEOPARDS, AND THE ELEPHANTS,' shouted a burly orang-utan, scrambling quickly to the bottom of the barrier.

'LOOK,' squealed a young doe, peering through a tiny gap in the barrier. 'They've brought hundreds of H-hyenas with them.'

Thousands of eyes of all sizes and colours peered through the barrier to see their enemies. It was a fearful sight.

Marching, grim-faced and growling low, fifty battalions of Law Leopards came within fifty metres of the barrier then stopped. With loud grunts their officers commanded them to spread out in formation. Behind the leopards, ten battalions of H-hyenas did the same.

Behind them, trumpeting loudly, two hundred of the biggest elephants in Allegoria waited impatiently.

When the leopards and H-hyenas, and the elephants had arrived, the parrots, doves, hummingbirds and macaws stopped their cacophony. Some of them moved higher into the trees for a safer view of the battle they knew was to come. Also, from all other parts of Allegoria thousands and thousands of Lo-clas and Ru-clas began to gather under the trees around the Swamplands to watch. Many of them were frightened.

All the leopards and a number of the H-hyena officers had coconut helmets tied firmly to their heads. Every leopard and H-hyena carried a baton, except the leader of the leopards, who now strutted forward a few paces.

Raising a megaphone to his mouth, he waited a few seconds before speaking, then roared: 'WE DO NOT WANT TO USE FORCE, BUT IF YOU DO NOT TAKE DOWN THIS BARRIER AT ONCE THEN I WILL ORDER MY LAW LEOPARDS AND H-HYENAS TO TEAR IT DOWN.'

'Just you try,' squeaked a tiny ring-tailed lemur from the top of the barrier, raising a sharp stick above his head.

'TAKE DOWN YOUR BARRIER,' the Law Leopard Leader insisted, ignoring the monkey's outburst. 'WE WILL NOT HARM YOU.' Lowering the megaphone, he waited to see what results his words would have.

A shrill warning from a curly-headed jungle fox called Ecan, rang out: 'Don't listen to him. Remember last night. Remember how they frightened us. Remember how they abused us. They will do worse if we take down our barrier. Don't think they will just return quietly to their headquarters if we take it down. No, they will attack us.'

With a scowl, the Leopard Leader raised his

megaphone again and snarled into it: 'THERE ARE EVIL TROUBLEMAKERS AMONGST YOU. THEY ARE USING YOU FOR THEIR EVIL PLANS. THEY ARE USING YOU,' he emphasised. He paused, waiting for a response. There was none. 'VERY WELL THEN, ON YOUR OWN HEADS BE IT. I WILL GIVE YOU FIVE MINUTES TO MAKE UP YOUR MINDS. THEN I WILL ORDER THE ELEPHANTS TO FLATTEN YOUR FORBIDDEN BARRIER. THEN WE WILL ENTER THE SWAMPLANDS AND ARREST YOU. YOU WILL ALL GO TO THE PIT.' He smiled wickedly as he heard the fearful gasps of some of the younger animals. 'FIVE MINUTES,' he roared, and with a sneer on his face he turned.

Just then a sharp stone, thrown by an over-active sloth on top of the barrier, hit him on his rump. With a loud squeal he leapt in the air, at the same time, wheeling to face the barrier.

Painfully he backed towards his Law Leopards.

Then it began. Stones, sharp sticks, thick thorns and other missiles began to fly at the leopards. Caught unawares by the ferocity of the attack, the leopards were driven back. Now hundreds of monkeys and other smaller animals swarmed over the barrier and down onto the ground and began to force the leopards back even further. The H-hyenas, laughing with fear, scattered and ran in terror for cover in the trees. Hundreds more animals joined the first wave over the barrier, but a hundred metres on in the trees, the leopards and the elephants began to muster.

'Look out. They're coming back,' screamed a tiny lizard.

'Quick, back inside the barrier,' shouted Ecan the fox.

Chattering loudly, the Swamplanders ran for the safety of the barrier. At the top of it hundreds of monkeys

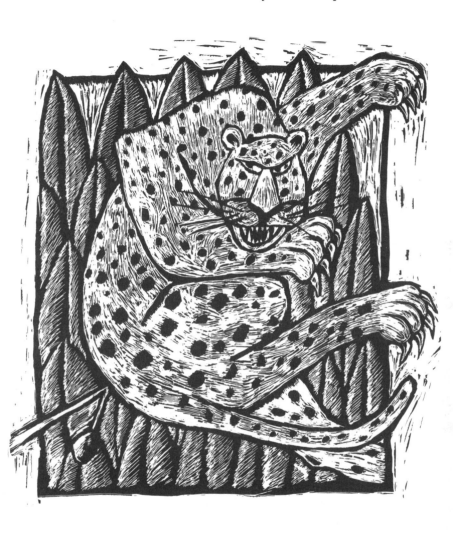

stopped and waited, stones and sticks clutched in their paws. Now, horrified, they saw several elephants with Law Leopards sitting on their broad backs thundering towards them.

'MORE STICKS . . . MORE STONES,' screamed Ecan. 'Hurry. Keep the monkeys supplied. The elephants must not get near the barrier. They'll flatten it . . . Hurry . . . hurry.'

As fast as they could, female monkeys, zebras and other animals formed a long line. Sticks and stones were passed from one to the other and right up to the monkeys on top of the barrier.

As the elephants thundered nearer, the monkeys let fly. Yelping with pain when they were hit, some of the leopards guiding the elephants leapt from their backs and scuttled back into the trees. Aiming carefully, the monkeys let loose another barrage of missiles. Now all the leopards leapt to safety. The elephants, having no one to guide them, stopped, unsure what to do.

'Drive them off, the elephants . . . Drive them off,' screamed Ecan the fox.

At once the monkeys let fly and sticks and stones thudded into the thick elephant hides. Trumpeting with pain they thundered back to the leopards.

'Hurrayyy . . . Hurrayyy . . . We've won . . . Hurrayyy,' shouted the Swamplanders. From the surrounding trees Ru-clas and Lo-clas cheered together.

'They're not beaten yet. Not by a long chalk,' shouted Ecan. 'They'll be back. We have to be ready for them. More stones and sticks. Be ready. They'll not give up . . . Hurry.'

A small female chimpanzee called Cli-na stared at Ecan. They'll not give up, she thought. No, they won't. I must get word to the Lions. As the others began to break off sticks, she hurried away to the far end of the

Swamplands to make contact with the messenger pigeons.

* * *

'What the blazes are we going to do?' laughed the leader of the H-hyenas. 'We'll never break through. There are too many of them.'

The leader of the leopards growled at him, then snarled, 'We'll break through alright . . . and when we do . . . when we do . . .' With a quick rip at the air, with his extended claws, he roared angrily.

* * *

'It won't be long before the Lions hear about this,' whispered old Emac, the zebra, as he and Bu-inn watched hundreds of Swamplanders passing ammunition along the line.

'Oh, they'll probably have heard by now,' Bu-inn smiled. 'And they'll not tolerate all this. They'll take action. It's a pity Chu-lain is missing it all.'

'He's in Nemedia isn't he?' Emac said.

'Aye, trouble has broken out there too.'

Both zebras watched as a female chimpanzee came running breathlessly back to the line. Then she bent and lifted a huge rock between her hairy paws. With a grunt she smashed it into another rock, splintering both of them into tiny pieces. A few macaws recorded all this and several other chimpanzees began to gather up the stones and carry them over to the barrier.

* * *

Meanwhile, far away across the water in Lionia, the

pigeon had arrived with word of what was happening in the Swamplands. The Lion King now paced up and down in front of his throne, speaking to his advisers.

'What is happening over there?' he finally growled, stopping and stretching himself, as he glared down at the group of lions who lay beneath his dais. 'Cannot the Ru-clas Lords control these . . . these Lo-clas Swamplanders? I will not allow any trouble in that part of my kingdom.' The Lion King's tiny gold crown bobbed about on top of his majestic head, as his yellow eyes gazed upon one of his advisers in particular.

'The Lo-clas started the trouble, your majesty. A Lo-clas zebra called Chu-lain. He was the one. With the help of some other zebras, he encouraged many Lo-clas to march through Allegoria. They are demanding one animal, one say. They also want better housing than the Ru-clas. The problem is, your majesty, that the Lo-clas actually think they are equal to the Ru-clas . . . and now the more impatient young jaguars and even some foxes are stirring up even more trouble.'

Suddenly the King's oldest adviser spoke, his voice thunderously hoarse: 'Actually, your majesty,' he said, his long grey mane bristling and his sharp claws moving in and out of his huge paws, 'it is a WHOLE HANDLIN'.'

'A WHAT?' roared the King, his long tail thumping up and down agitatedly. 'What did you say? A WHOLE HANDLIN'? . . . I can't allow a WHOLE HANDLIN' to take place in any part of my kingdom.' He glared at his wisest adviser. 'Are you sure it is a WHOLE HANDLIN'?'

'Yes, your majesty.'

The King of Lionia and Allegoria glared: 'Well then,' he snapped. 'What do you suggest I should do about this . . . this WHOLE HANDLIN'?'

The old adviser's face, creasing into many wrinkles,

said: 'I would never have the audacity to suggest anything your majesty. However, if I were the wise King you are, I would send a battalion of the Royal Army to quell this trouble. The Lo-clas would welcome your army. They will be grateful to you . . . and more importantly, they will be loyal to you. A wise move, I think, your majesty.'

Narrowing his eyes, the King began to pace up and down as he thought about this. A minute later he stopped. Then he crawled up onto the great throne and boomed: 'Very well. Send one thousand of my royal Lion Army. Tell them to quell this trouble quickly. Tell them to make friends with these Lo-clas, especially the zebras who started it all.'

* * *

Meanwhile, the Swamplanders were ready for another attack.

'THEY'RE USING THE ELEPHANTS AGAIN,' screamed a monkey lookout from the tree just beyond the barrier. Squinting through the barrier, Ecan saw that the Law Leopards were indeed using the elephants. In a long line, three-deep, and with the H-hyenas bringing up the rear, the leopards were prodding the angry trumpeting elephants towards the barrier.

'What'll we do now?' cried a young doe, her beautiful body trembling with fear.

What will we do, thought Ecan, watching several mice and rats struggling as they carried a huge rock to the bottom of the barrier. Then it came to him. 'The mice,' he shouted, his face breaking into a crafty smile. 'all the mice, where are they? Get them here at once. Hurry.'

Within ten seconds hundreds of mice, their noses wrinkling with puzzlement, gathered around the fox.

'Now,' Ecan said, addressing them, 'you know the

elephants will panic if they see you. Elephants are afraid of mice, therefore, I want you to slip through the barrier and run towards the elephants. You are too quick for the leopards to catch so you have nothing to worry about. Frighten the elephants. Turn them back. Don't let them get near the barrier. Do you all understand what you have to do?'

The mice stared at Ecan for a few moments, then with excited smiles on their faces they slipped through the narrow gaps in the barrier and scooted towards the approaching elephants. At first, in their mad rush, the elephants didn't see the mice. Then suddenly, with a loud fearful trumpet, the leader of the elephants reared in the air, waving his two thick front paws in front of him. He raised his trunk straight up and his tiny eyes widened with fear. All the other elephants stopped.

'On . . . on,' screamed the Law Leopards, prodding harder at the elephants' legs. 'Why have you stopped? Go on.'

Now other elephants saw the mice and in a panic they turned, their big ears flopping about as they began to run faster and faster, stampeding through the leopards and H-hyenas, crushing several of them under foot, before crashing into the trees.

'Now!' screamed Ecan. 'Up and at them.'

With loud cheers a thousand animals scrambled up and over the barrier and began to attack the leopards and the H-hyenas.

'Retreat . . . fall back,' screamed the leader of the leopards as a stone hit him on the side of his neck.

In seconds the leopards and the H-hyenas turned and fled after the elephants into the cover of the trees. A great cheer went up, and the Swampland mice scuttled back behind the barrier.

'They're not beaten yet,' Ecan said, as he patted several

monkeys on the back. 'They'll be back, but not for a while. It's growing dark. We have time to get better prepared. Gather up more stones. Break off more sticks. We must be ready for the next round.'

9

Saved

It was now almost dark and the jungle throbbed with the sounds of the night creatures. Deep in the trees just beyond the Swamplands the leopard officers and the leader of the H-hyenas sat in a tiny clearing discussing their battle plans.

'It's a waste of time to try anything now. The Lo-clas would have the advantage in the darkness,' one of the leopard officers snarled.

'We'll never be able to break down their barrier using the elephants anyway,' another leopard officer growled. 'The second they see the mice they'd panic.'

At this the leader of the H-hyenas' ears pricked up and, rising to his feet, he laughed out loud. 'That's it.'

The leopards stared at him.

'The second the elephants see the mice they panic. Well, what if the elephants couldn't see the mice, eh? What then? What would happen if the elephants' long ears were tied in front of their eyes? What then? We could guide them forward. They'd be blindfolded. They wouldn't see the mice. They wouldn't be afraid.

The leader of the leopards gaped at the H-hyena for a few seconds, then his face broke into a smile. 'Blindfold the elephants. Why, why that's a brilliant idea.'

Now the other leopards stared suspiciously at the blushing H-hyena leader.

Then the leopard leader asked: 'Where are you getting so much GUMPTION from, H-hyena?'

'GUMPTION?' the H-hyena laughed nervously. 'Why it just came to me. I don't know, but it just came to me.'

Once again the leopard leader studied the H-hyena leader, then turning he snapped at the leopards: 'Well, it's a good idea, isn't it?'

They all nodded, their eyes still on the H-hyena.

'Right then, here's what we'll do. We will blindfold the elephants with their floppy ears and guide them into the barrier. Then when we have flattened it we will overrun the Swamplands and give the Lo-clas a lesson they will never forget.' The leader was satisfied.

'Yeahhhh,' roared the leopards and the H-hyena happily.

Sniffing the air, the Law Leopard Leader looked up into the sky, then said, 'We'll abandon all attacks until early morning. At dawn we attack, and this time the Lo-clas will not be able to stop us.'

Later, laughing hysterically, the leader of the H-hyenas slipped away to tell his officers about his great idea.

＊　＊　＊

As dawn slipped quickly over the jungle and the birds began their chorus, the animals lying under the trees surrounding the Swamplands awoke. Side-by-side all night, the Lo-clas and Ru-clas had slept, and now side-by-side they stood to see the final battle.

In the Swamplands Ecan climbed to the top of the barrier. His sharp eyes narrowed as he squinted into the mist-shrouded trees. He could hear the sounds of the elephants. What are they up to, he thought. Surely the

leopards know using the elephants would be a useless
ploy. The answer came sooner than expected.

Suddenly, crashing through the trees, came two
hundred elephants with their ears tied in front of their
eyes. On top of each elephant's back were two leopards
and two H-hyenas.

Ecan's eyes widened with horror as he leapt to the
bottom of the barrier. 'They're attacking . . . they're
attacking,' he screamed. 'They've blindfolded the
elephants. The mice won't work now.'

'We're lost,' squeaked several mice, their voices just
audible above the sounds of the trumpeting elephants.

'No . . . we're not lost,' screamed Ecan. 'Don't let me
hear talk like that. We can still drive them off.' Swinging
towards the animals who were standing shocked at the
bottom of the barrier he roared: 'Come on you lot. Get
more sticks and stones up to your comrades on top.
Hurry . . . hurry.' Then he shouted up to the monkeys on
top of the barrier as the other animals formed a line: 'Aim
for the H-hyenas. They're the ones guiding the
elephants.'

Already a line of animals supplying the monkeys
stretched one hundred metres.

'On . . . on . . . ' screamed the leopard officers, and
onward thundered the elephants. At the front of the
attack four of the biggest elephants were left without
guidance as the sticks and stones rained on their guiders.
With wild leaps the H-hyenas leapt from the elephants'
backs, and the leopards followed them, dodging out of
the way of the other elephants as they came on. The
ground shook and in the Swamplands several smaller
animals found it hard to stay on their paws. Suddenly,
two elephants managed to reach the barrier. The air was
thick with missiles and as the H-hyenas and the leopards
leapt to safety, the two huge creatures hit the barrier.

Chattering with fear, fifty monkeys toppled from the top of it. Now Ecan and the animals down below could see that the barrier was badly damaged. This shock was followed by another, then another, as more elephants hit the barrier. Horrified now, the Swamplanders saw that the barrier was finished. From the surrounding trees the animals stared worriedly. Now all but a few branches were left to hold the barrier together. Then four more elephants collided into these and it was all over.

The leader of the leopards roared for his megaphone to be brought to him.

'STOP . . . CEASE . . . THE BARRIER IS DOWN. WITHDRAW THE ELEPHANTS. WE HAVE WON. THE BARRIER IS DOWN.'

As the H-hyenas guided the elephants away, the leopard leader grinned triumphantly. Then he strode forward. Hundreds of his Law Leopards marched behind him, their open mouths dripping saliva as they thought about the slaughter that was to come. As they drew nearer they salivated even more, for they smelled the Swamplanders' fear. In the trees the watching Lo-clas and Ru-clas held their breaths as they realised they were about to witness slaughter. The macaws and parrots were silent, and some of them even flew away, unable to record the scene.

At long last, thought the leader of the leopards, we will wipe out these Lo-clas. Destroy them as an example to all the Lo-clas and any of our own Ru-clas who might have soft ideas. With a smile he withdrew his baton and raised it above his head, ready to give the signal for his Law Leopards to attack. Many of the animals in the trees began to cry. The animals in the Swamplands were too terrified to move.

Suddenly every animal within fifty miles heard the roar of the Lions.

'STAND STILL. DO NOT MOVE. BY ORDER OF THE KING OF ALL THE JUNGLES,' roared the leader of the Royal Lions. 'DO NOT ATTACK THE SWAMPLANDERS.'

'It's the Lions from Lionia,' shouted Cli-na happily. 'They've come to save us . . . Hurrayyy . . . Hurrayyy.'

Then all the animals in the Swamplands and in the trees began to cheer. 'Hurrayyy . . . Hurrayyy . . .'

With a terrible scowl on his face, the Law Leopard Leader lowered his baton as he saw one thousand of the strongest and fiercest lions push aside his Law Leopards and H-hyenas and march into the Swamplands. The Leopard Leader's claws tore into his baton as he saw the happy welcome the Swamplanders gave the lions. Some female animals even began to carry out food and water to them.

After the welcome had died down the leader of the Royal Lions growled loudly to the leader of the Law Leopards for all to hear: 'From now on, Leopard, you will take orders from me. There will be no more attacks. The WHOLE HANDLIN' is over. My orders from the King are to take command of Allegoria until jungle order and jungle law is restored. Also, there will be an investigation into all this.'

Fuming with anger, but afraid, the Leopard Leader snarled: 'The Low-clas are evil troublemakers. It was they who started it. Now is your chance to beat them down. They must never . . . .'

With a mighty roar that terrified all the leopards, the leader of the Royal Lions interrupted saying: 'You will obey me. Take your leopards and return to your headquarters. And stay there. We will take over now. There will be no more trouble. Now, go, . . . GO!' Rearing above the terrified leopard's head the lion pawed the air angrily. 'Go!' he roared again.

Trembling, the leopard slunk back and with his tail between his legs, growled orders for his Law Leopards and the H-hyenas to return to headquarters. As they marched away, the Swamplanders and the animals under the trees cheered more loudly than they had ever cheered before.

Long after the leopards and the H-hyenas had gone, Ecan watched the welcome the Royal Army were receiving. I hope, he thought, these royal saviours do not turn out to be the enemy after a while. Then with a quiet angry bark, the wily fox slipped out of the Swamplands and into the trees.

10

Was it all Worthwhile?

That night the meeting that took place in the great hall at Em-hain was a stormy one. All the jungle lords were there as well as the leopard officers and their leader.

'And now,' shouted a tall giraffe lord called Cian, 'that old fool, Emac, has asked the Royal Lions to hold an enquiry into why the WHOLE HANDLIN' started, and it's all your fault too.

'What?' Tigern-mas snarled, angry and astonished at the outburst from one of his most faithful followers. 'What do you mean it was my fault? How was I to know the Lions had been sent for? How was I to know they would interfere?'

'It is your fault,' roared Cu-roi pushing to the front of the hall. 'I warned you all,' he said, glaring at Ath-ach. 'But you wouldn't listen. Now, before you all I take my rightful place as your new leader. It was witnessed and agreed.' He glared triumphantly at the scowling Ath-ach.

At this Ath-ach thumped his chest loudly and roared: 'I object to this. It was not Tigern-mas's fault. It was his.' Swinging around he pointed a stubby forefinger at the leader of the leopards. 'He handled the whole thing stupidly.'

The leopard leader's jaw fell open with shock as he listened to Ath-ach condemn his tactics. 'But . . . I . . . I did my best,' he stammered.

'Well it was not good enough, and now look at the mess we are all in,' shouted Ath-ach.

'Ath-ach,' Cu-roi shouted, his neck bristling with anger, 'it was as much your fault as it was Tigern-mas's. You can't make a scapegoat out of the leopard leader. There is only one thing to do now, and as your new leader I will see it is done.' The three Tiger Lords and the other lords and leopards nodded in agreement as Cu-roi said: 'The Lo-clas want one animal, one say. They will have it. How can that harm us?'

'I'll tell you how it can harm us,' bellowed Ath-ach, hatred for the Giraffe Lord Cu-roi burning from his bulging bloodshot eyes. 'It can make them think they are as good as us. They . . .'

'ALSO,' Cu-roi said in a louder voice than Ath-ach's. 'We will set up a housing programme. Give them better houses. It shouldn't be too difficult to arrange that. Develop the Swamplands. The Lo-clas like it there.' Now Cu-roi paused for a few seconds before adding, 'Well, what do you think? Do you all agree? Or are you going to listen to the splutterings of Ath-ach? Ah look my friends, we have to give in. This division between the Lo-clas and the Ru-clas cannot go on forever. We have to meet them halfway.' He smiled as he looked around the hall, ignoring Ath-ach's fierce glare. 'Well, what do you say?'

'I choose Cu-roi as my new leader and I accept anything that he proposes to save Allegoria from more trouble,' shouted Cian, his long neck moving up and down with excitement.

'Aye, me too,' growled the leopard leader, giving Ath-ach an extremely dirty look. He failed to see Cu-roi wink slyly at one of his officers.

Soon the hall resounded with shouts, backing Cu-roi. Furious now, Ath-ach glowered at Tigern-mas, who lowered his eyes. Then with a loud roar Ath-ach said: 'Let me tell you this, Cu-roi. If you allow the Lo-clas to have one animal, one say, then I vow . . . I VOW . . . I will bring you down. Some day, somehow, I will get all the Ru-clas behind me. The next time I come into this hall it will be as your new leader. I am the only animal in all of Allegoria who can restore Ru-clas pride.' Thumping his chest repeatedly he stormed from the hall.

Several jungle lords followed him.

Epilogue

In the following years the trouble in Allegoria grew worse, flaring up every few days, each incident more serious than the one before.

One fine summer day, Chu-lain, Tua-tal, and Bu-inn were sunning themselves by their favourite water-hole. They watched lazily as a flock of geese landed on the still water. With loud squawks they waved their strong white wings at their three favourite zebras.

'It only seems like yesterday,' sighed Chu-lain, 'that old Emac sat here with us planning that first march.'

'Aye, it does,' Tua-tal said, sadly, shaking his grey head. 'Still, he died knowing that the Lo-class would never again think of themselves as second-class animals.'

'Yes,' Bu-inn said. 'He was a good example to us. I'm glad though that he isn't alive to see what is happening now.'

Sniffing sadly, Chu-lain whispered, 'One thing they can't take away from us is one animal, one say. Emac was proud of the fact that he led the march to win that.'

'Yes he was,' Bu-inn said. 'But, Chu-lain, was it all worthwhile? When you remember all the Lo-clas, and Ru-clas, Law Leopards and Lions who have died, would you do it all again?'

Chu-lain stared at his friend. Had it all been worthwhile, he thought. He didn't know. Many changes had followed that first squat with Ja-no and Mo-li. But now his GUMPTION was waning, for he could see no end to the troubles in Allegoria. He sighed heavily as Bu-inn's question came to him again. WAS IT ALL WORTHWHILE?